Praise for

TEMPT ME AT TWILIGHT

"Enchanting romance…Lisa Kleypas has created a cast of characters that could keep readers enthralled for years."
—*Chicago Tribune*

"Brimming with superbly nuanced characters, simmering sexual chemistry, and wicked wit, the latest in Kleypas's Victorian-set Hathaway series is a thoroughly romantic literary treat."
—*Booklist*

"From the first page to the last of her latest Hathaway novel, Kleypas delivers a witty, charming (wait until you meet the animals!), vibrant, sensual love story that takes your breath away. Her unique storytelling shines as she creates situations that elicit powerful emotions. Best of all, just when you think you know what's going to happen, she surprises you in this deep-sigh story."
—*Romantic Times BOOKreviews*

"A delectable story with a hero and heroine to savor. It's a fine addition to the Hathaway family series."
—*Romance Reader*

"An absolute delight."
—*Night Owl Romance*

MORE…

SEDUCE ME AT SUNRISE

"Has plenty to keep readers turning the pages: wit, suspense, secrets to learn, and, of course, lots of love and passion."
                                                                    —*The Monitor*

"Each member of the family is a delight to meet, and the depths of emotions and love they have for each other are shown magnificently...a spectacular story that continues the saga of the Hathaway family."
                                                                    —*Romance Reviews*

"Lushly sexy and thoroughly romantic...superbly crafted characters and an intriguing plot blend together brilliantly in this splendid romance."   —*Booklist*

MINE TILL MIDNIGHT

"Vintage Kleypas...An unforgettable story peopled with remarkable characters and a depth of emotion that will leave you breathless with the wonderment of knowing what falling in love is really like."
                                                                    —*Romantic Times BOOKreviews*

"Kleypas's effortless style makes for another sexy exploration of 19th-century passion and peccadilloes, riveting from start to finish."   —*Publishers Weekly*

Also by
LISA KLEYPAS

WALLFLOWER SERIES
Scandal in Spring

Devil in Winter

It Happened One Autumn

Secrets of a Summer Night

TEXAS TRILOGY
Sugar Daddy

Blue-Eyed Devil

Smooth Talking Stranger

THE HATHAWAYS
Mine Till Midnight

Seduce Me at Sunrise

Tempt Me at Twilight

Married by Morning

Love in the Afternoon

A
WALLFLOWER
CHRISTMAS

LISA KLEYPAS

St. Martin's Paperbacks

This is a work of fiction. All of the characters, organizations, and events portrayed in this novel are either products of the author's imagination or are used fictitiously.

A WALLFLOWER CHRISTMAS

Copyright © 2008 by Lisa Kleypas.
Excerpt from *Christmas Eve at Friday Harbor* copyright © 2010 by Lisa Kleypas.

Cover photograph © Alan Ayers
Cover design by Elizabeth Connor and Brendan Dalton

For information address St. Martin's Press, 175 Fifth Avenue, New York, NY 10010.

Library of Congress Catalog Card Number: 2008024270

ISBN: 978-0-312-36073-3

Printed in the United States of America

St. Martin's hardcover edition / October 2008
St. Martin's Paperbacks edition / November 2010

St. Martin's Paperbacks are published by St. Martin's Press, 175 Fifth Avenue, New York, NY 10010.

10 9 8 7 6 5 4 3 2 1

To Jennifer Enderlin,
who has so many personal graces;
wisdom, talent, beauty, and generosity of spirit.
Thank you for bringing so much joy
to my life and my work.

Love always,
LK

PROLOGUE

Once there were four young ladies who sat at the side of every ball, soiree, and party during the London season. Waiting night after night in a row of chairs, the wallflowers eventually struck up a conversation. They realized that although they were in competition for the same group of gentlemen, there was more to be gained from being friends rather than adversaries. And even more than that, they liked one another. They decided to band together to find husbands, starting with the oldest, Annabelle, and working down to the youngest, Daisy.

Annabelle was unquestionably the most beautiful wallflower, but she was virtually penniless, which put her at the greatest disadvantage. Although most London bachelors hoped for a wife with a pretty face, they usually settled for one with a handsome dowry.

Evie was unconventionally attractive, with flaming hair and abundant freckles. It was well-known that someday she would inherit a fortune from her father. However, her father was a common-born ex-boxer who owned a gambling club, and such a disreputable background was a difficult obstacle for a young lady to surmount. Even worse, Evie was cripplingly shy and had a stammer. Any man who tried to talk to her would later describe the encounter as an act of torture.

Lillian and Daisy were sisters from New York. Their family, the Bowmans, were astonishingly, vulgarly, almost unimaginably wealthy, having made their fortune with a soap-manufacturing business. They had no good blood, no manners, and no social patrons. Lillian was a fiercely loving friend, but also strong-willed and bossy. And Daisy was a dreamer who often fretted that real life was never quite as interesting as the novels she read so voraciously.

As the wallflowers helped one another navigate the perils of London society, and consoled and supported one another through very real dangers, sorrows, and joys, they each found a husband, and no one referred to them as wallflowers anymore.

In every social season, however, there was no shortage of new wallflowers. (Then, as now, there were always girls who were overlooked and ignored by gentlemen who really should have known better.)

But then there was the Christmas when Rafe Bowman, Lillian and Daisy's oldest brother, came to England. After that, life for one London wallflower would never be the same. . . .

ONE

London 1845

"It's official," Lillian, Lady Westcliff, said with satisfaction, setting aside the letter from her brother. "Rafe will reach London in precisely a fortnight. And the clipper's name is the *Whirlwind,* which I think is quite apt in light of his impending betrothal."

She glanced down at Annabelle and Evie, who were both on the parlor floor working on a massive circle of red velvet. They had gathered at Lillian's London house, Marsden Terrace, for an afternoon of tea and conversation.

At the moment Annabelle and Evie were making a tree skirt, or rather trying to salvage the fabric from Lillian's previous efforts. Evie was snipping at a piece of brocade ribbon that had been stitched unevenly on one side, while Annabelle was busy cutting a new edge of fabric and pinning it.

The only one missing was Lillian's younger sister, Daisy, who lived in Bristol with her new husband.

Annabelle longed to see Daisy and find out how marriage suited her. Thankfully they would all be together soon for the Christmas holiday in Hampshire.

"Do you think your brother will have any difficulty convincing Lady Natalie to marry him?" Annabelle asked, frowning as she encountered a large, dark stain on the fabric.

"Oh, not at all," Lillian said breezily. "He's handsome, charming, and very rich. What could Lady Natalie possibly object to, aside from the fact that he's an American?"

"Well, Daisy said he's a rake. And some young women might not—"

"Nonsense!" Lillian exclaimed. "Rafe is not at all a rake. Oh, he's sown a few oats, but what red-blooded man hasn't?"

Annabelle regarded her doubtfully. Although Lillian's younger sister Daisy was generally regarded as a dreamer and a romantic, she had a streak of clear-eyed pragmatism that made her judgments quite reliable. If Daisy had said their oldest brother was a rake, there was undoubtedly strong evidence to support the assertion.

"Does he drink and gamble?" Annabelle asked Lillian.

A wary frown. "On occasion."

"Does he behave in rude or improper ways?"

"He's a Bowman. We don't know any better."

"Does he pursue women?"

"Of course."

"Has he ever been faithful to one woman? Has he ever fallen in love?"

Lillian frowned at her. "Not that I'm aware of."

Annabelle glanced at Evie with raised brows. "What do you think, Evie?"

"Rake," came the succinct reply.

"Oh, all right," Lillian grumbled. "I suppose he is a rake. But that may not be an impediment to his courtship of Lady Natalie. Some women like rakes. Look at Evie."

Evie continued to snip doggedly through the brocade ribbon, while a smile curved her lips. "I don't l-like *all* rakes," she said, her gaze on her work. "Just one."

Evie, the gentlest and most soft-spoken of them all, had been the one least likely to capture the heart of the notorious Lord St. Vincent, who had been the *definitive* rake. Although Evie, with her round blue eyes and blazing red hair, possessed a rare and unconventional beauty, she was unbearably shy. And there was the stammer. But Evie also had a reserve of quiet strength and a gallant spirit that seemed to have seduced her husband utterly.

"And that former rake obviously adores you beyond reason," Annabelle said. She paused, studying Evie intently before asking softly, "Is St. Vincent pleased about the baby, dear?"

"Oh, yes, he's—" Evie broke off and gave Annabelle a wide-eyed glance of surprise. "How did you know?"

Annabelle grinned. "I've noticed your new gowns all have front and back pleats that can be let out as your figure expands. It's an instant giveaway, dear."

"You're expecting?" Lillian asked, letting out a tomboyish whoop of delight. She launched off the settee and dropped beside Evie, throwing her long arms around her.

"That is *capital* news! How are you feeling? Are you queasy yet?"

"Only when I saw what you had done to the tree skirt," Evie said, laughing at her friend's exuberance. It was often difficult to remember that Lillian was a countess. Her spontaneous nature had not been subdued one whit by her new social prominence.

"Oh, you should *not* be on the floor," Lillian exclaimed. "Here, give me the scissors, and I'll work on this dratted thing—"

"No," Evie and Annabelle said at the same time.

"Lillian, dear," Annabelle continued firmly, "you are not to come anywhere near this tree skirt. What you do with a needle and thread should be considered a criminal act."

"I do try," Lillian protested with a lopsided grin, settling back on her heels. "I start out with such good intentions, but then I get tired of making all those tiny stitches, and I start to hurry through it. But we *must* have a tree skirt, a very large one. Otherwise there will be nothing to catch the drips of wax when the tree candles are lit."

"Would you mind telling me what this stain is from?" Annabelle pointed to a dark ugly splotch on the velvet.

Lillian's grin turned sheepish. "I thought perhaps we could arrange that part in the back. I spilled a glass of wine on it."

"You were drinking while sewing?" Annabelle asked, thinking that explained quite a lot.

"I hoped it would help me to relax. Sewing makes me nervous."

Annabelle gave her a quizzical smile. "Why?"

"It reminds me of all the times my mother would stand over me while I worked on my sampler. And whenever I made a mistake, she rapped my knuckles with a ruler." Lillian gave a self-deprecating grin, but for once the amusement didn't reach her lively brown eyes. "I was a terrible child."

"You were a dear child, I'm sure," Annabelle said gently. She had never been quite certain how Lillian and Daisy Bowman had turned out so well, given their upbringing. Thomas and Mercedes Bowman somehow managed to be demanding, critical, *and* neglectful, which was quite a feat.

Three years earlier the Bowmans had brought their two daughters to London after discovering that even their great fortune could not induce anyone from the New York upper circles to marry the girls.

Through a combination of hard work, luck, and a necessary ruthlessness, Thomas Bowman had established one of the largest and fastest-growing soap companies in the world. Now that soap was becoming affordable for the masses, the Bowmans' manufactories in New York and Bristol could scarcely keep up with the demand.

It took more than money, however, to achieve a place in New York society. Heiresses of undistinguished bloodlines, such as Lillian and Daisy, were not at all desirable to their male counterparts, who also wanted to marry up. Therefore London, with its ever-growing pool of impoverished aristocrats, was fertile hunting ground for American *nouveaux riches*.

With Lillian, ironically, the Bowmans had reached their highest pinnacle in having married her to Marcus,

Lord Westcliff. No one could have believed that the reserved and powerful earl would wed a headstrong girl like Lillian. But Westcliff had seen beneath Lillian's brash façade to the vulnerability and fiercely loving heart she tried so hard to conceal.

"I was a hellion," Lillian said frankly, "and so was Rafe. Our other brothers, Ransom and Rhys, were always a bit better behaved, although that's not saying much. And Daisy would take part in my troublemaking, but most of the time she daydreamed and lived in her books."

"Lillian," Annabelle asked, carefully rolling a length of ribbon, "why has your brother agreed to meet with Lady Natalie and the Blandfords? Is he truly ready to marry? Has he need of the money, or is he seeking to please your father?"

"I'm not certain," Lillian said. "I don't think it's the money. Rafe has made a fortune in Wall Street speculations, some of them a bit unscrupulous. I suspect he may finally have tired of being at loggerheads with Father. Or perhaps . . ." She hesitated, a shadow crossing her face.

"Perhaps?" Evie prompted softly.

"Well, Rafe affects a carefree façade, but he has never been a terribly happy person. Mother and Father were abominable to him. To all of us, really. They would never let us play with anyone they thought was beneath us. And they thought *everyone* was beneath us. The twins had each other, and of course Daisy and I were always together. But Rafe was always alone. Father wanted him to be a serious-minded boy, so Rafe was kept isolated from other children. Rafe was never allowed to do anything that Father considered frivolous."

"So he eventually rebelled," Annabelle said.

Lillian grinned briefly. "Oh, yes." Her amusement faded. "But now I wonder . . . what happens when a young man is tired of being serious, and also tired of rebelling? What's left after that?"

"Apparently we'll find out."

"I want him to be happy," Lillian said. "To find someone he could care about."

Evie regarded them both thoughtfully. "Has anyone actually *met* Lady Natalie? Do we know anyth-thing about her character?"

"I haven't met her," Lillian admitted, "but she has a wonderful reputation. She's a sheltered girl who came out in society last year and was quite sought after. I've heard she is lovely and exceedingly well bred." She paused and made a face. "Rafe will frighten her to death. God knows why the Blandfords are advocating the marriage. It must be that they need the money. Father would pay anything to pump more blue blood into the family."

"I wish we could speak with s-someone who is acquainted with her," Evie mused. "Someone who might advise your brother, give him little hints about things she likes, her f-favorite flowers, that sort of thing."

"She has a companion," Lillian volunteered. "A poor cousin named Hannah-something. I wonder if we could invite her to tea before Rafe meets Lady Natalie?"

"I think that's a splendid idea," Annabelle exclaimed.

"If she's even a little forthcoming about Lady Natalie, it could help Rafe's case immensely."

"Yes, you must go," Lord Blandford said decisively.

Hannah stood before him in the parlor of the Blandford home in Mayfair. It was one of the smaller, older houses in the fashionable residential district, tucked in a little enclave near Hyde Park on the west.

Comprised of handsome squares and broad thoroughfares, Mayfair was home to many privileged aristocratic families. But in the past decade there had been new development in the area, oversized mansions and towering Gothic-style houses cropping up in the north, where the recently moneyed class was establishing itself.

"Do anything you can," Blandford continued, "to help facilitate an attachment between my daughter and Mr. Bowman."

Hannah stared at him in disbelief. Lord Blandford had always been a man of discernment and taste. She could scarcely believe that he would want Natalie, his only child, to be married off to a crass American manufacturer's son. Natalie was beautiful, polished, and mature beyond her twenty years. She could have any man she chose.

"Uncle," Hannah said carefully, "I would never dream of questioning your judgment, but—"

"But you want to know if I've taken leave of my senses?" he asked, and chuckled as she nodded. He gestured to the upholstered armchair on the other side of the hearth. "Have a seat, my dear."

They did not often have the opportunity to speak

privately. But Lady Blandford and Natalie were visiting a cousin who had taken ill, and it had been decided that Hannah would remain in London to prepare Natalie's clothes and personal items for the upcoming holiday in Hampshire.

Staring into the wise, kind face of the man who had been so generous to her, Hannah asked, "May I speak frankly, Uncle?"

His eyes twinkled at that. "I have never known you to speak otherwise, Hannah."

"Yes, well . . . I showed you Lady Westcliff's invitation to tea as a courtesy, but I had not intended to accept it."

"Why not?"

"Because the only reason they would want to invite me is to ferret out information about Natalie, and also to impress me with all the supposed virtues of Mr. Bowman. And Uncle, it is obvious that Lady Westcliff's brother is not nearly good enough for Natalie!"

"It appears he has been tried and convicted already," Lord Blandford said mildly. "Are you so severe upon Americans, Hannah?"

"It's not that he's American," Hannah protested. "Or at least, that's not his fault. But his culture, his values, his appetites are entirely foreign to someone like Natalie. She could never be happy with him."

"Appetites?" Blandford asked, raising his brows.

"Yes, for money and power. And although he is a person of consequence in New York, he has no rank here. Natalie isn't used to that. It's an awkward match."

"You're right, of course," Blandford surprised her by saying. He settled back in his chair, weaving his fingers

together. Blandford was a pleasant, placid-faced man,
his head large and well shaped, the bald skin hugging
his skull tightly and then draping in more relaxed folds
around his eyes, cheeks, and jowls. The substantial
framework of his body was lank and bony, as if nature
had forgotten to weave the necessary amount of muscle
to support his skeleton.

"It is an awkward match in some regards," Blandford
continued. "But it may be the saving of future generations of the family. My dear, you are very nearly a daughter to me, so I will speak bluntly. There is no son to
inherit the title after me, and I will not leave Natalie and
Lady Blandford to the questionable generosity of the
next Lord Blandford. They must be provided for. To my
profound regret, I will not be able to leave a satisfactory
income for them, as most of the Blandford monies and
lands are entailed."

"But there are Englishmen of means who would
dearly love to marry Natalie. Lord Travers, for example.
He and Natalie share a great affinity, and he has generous means at his disposal—"

"*Acceptable* means," Blandford corrected quietly.
"Not generous. And nothing close to what Bowman
has now, not to mention his future inheritance."

Hannah was bewildered. In all the years she had
known Lord Blandford, he had never displayed an outward concern for wealth. It was not done among men of
his station, who disdained conversations about finance
as bourgeois and far beneath them. What had prompted
this worry over money?

Reading her expression, Blandford smiled morosely.
"Ah, Hannah. How can I explain adequately? The world

is moving altogether too fast for men like me. Too many new ways of doing things. Before I can adjust to the way something changes, it changes yet again. They say before long the railway will cover every green acre of England. The masses will all have soap and tinned food and ready-made clothing, and the distance between us and them will grow quite narrow."

Hannah listened intently, aware that she, with her lack of fortune and undistinguished birth, straddled the line between Blandford's own class and "the masses."

"Is that a bad thing, Uncle?"

"Not entirely," Blandford said after a long hesitation. "Though I do regret that blood and gentility are coming to mean so little. The future is upon us, and it belongs to climbers like the Bowmans. And to men like Lord Westcliff, who are willing to sacrifice what they must to keep pace with it."

The earl of Westcliff was Raphael Bowman's brother-in-law. He had arguably the most distinguished lineage in England, with blood more blue than the Queen's. And yet he was known as a progressive, both politically and financially. Among his many investments, Westcliff had garnered a fortune from the development of the locomotive industry, and he was said to take a keen interest in mercantile matters. All this while most of the peerage was still content to garner its profits from the centuries-old tradition of maintaining tenants on its private lands.

"Then you desire the connection to Lord Westcliff, as well as the Bowmans," Hannah said.

"Of course. It will put my daughter in a unique position, marrying a wealthy American *and* having a brother-in-law such as Westcliff. As the wife of a Bowman, she will be seated at the lower end of the table . . . but it will be Westcliff's table, and that is no small consideration."

"I see," she said pensively.

"But you don't agree?"

No. Hannah was far from persuaded that her beloved Natalie should have to make do with an ill-mannered boor as a husband, merely to have Lord Westcliff as a brother-in-law. However, she was certainly not going to impugn Lord Blandford's judgment. At least not aloud.

"I defer to your wisdom, Uncle. However, I do hope that the advantages—or disadvantages—of this match will reveal themselves quickly."

A quiet laugh escaped him. "What a diplomat you are. You have a shrewd mind, my dear. Probably more than a young woman has need of. Better to be pretty and empty-headed like my daughter, than plain and clever."

Hannah did not take offense, although she could have argued both points. For one thing, her cousin Natalie was anything but empty-headed. However, Natalie knew better than to flaunt her intelligence, as that was not a quality that attracted suitors.

And Hannah did not consider herself plain. She was brown-haired and green-eyed, and she had a nice smile and a decent figure. If Hannah had the benefit of lovely clothes and adornments, she thought she might be considered very appealing. It was all in the eye of the beholder.

"Go to tea at Marsden Terrace," Lord Blandford told her, smiling. "Sow the seeds of romance. A match must be made. And as the Bard so aptly put it, 'The world must be peopled.'" He glanced at her significantly. "After we manage to marry off Natalie, you will no doubt find your own suitor. I have my suspicions about you and Mr. Clark, you see."

Hannah felt color rising in her face. For the past year she had undertaken some minor secretarial duties for Samuel Clark, a close friend and distant relation of Lord Blandford's. And Hannah entertained some private hopes regarding the attractive bachelor, who was fair-haired and slim and not much older than she. But perhaps her hopes were not as private as she had thought. "I'm sure I don't know what you mean, Uncle."

"I'm sure you do," he said, and chuckled. "All in good time, my dear. First let us secure a satisfactory future for Natalie. And then it will be your turn."

Hannah smiled at him, keeping her thoughts private. But inwardly she knew that her definition of a "satisfactory future" for Natalie was not quite the same as his. Natalie deserved a man who would be a loving, responsible, trustworthy husband.

And if Rafe Bowman were that man, he would have to prove it.

TWO

"At the risk of sounding arrogant," Rafe said, "I don't think I need advice about how to court a woman."

Rafe had arrived in London the day before. Today, while Westcliff was off visiting the locomotive works in which he had a share, Rafe gathered he was supposed to have tea with Lillian and her friends.

Rafe would have preferred to tour the locomotive works. He was a manufacturer's son, and the lure of new machines and gadgetry held an unending fascination for him. On the other hand, Lillian had asked him to stay, and he had never been able to refuse her anything. He adored his sisters, who in his opinion were the best things his parents had ever accomplished.

"Miss Appleton is not going to give you advice," Lillian retorted, ruffling his hair fondly. "We've invited her to tea so that she can tell us more about Lady Natalie. I should think you'd like to find out as much as you can about your future bride."

"That's still in question," Rafe reminded her wryly. "Even if I want to marry her, it's still left to Lady Natalie to consider whether she'll have me."

"Which is why you're going to be *so* charming that Miss Appleton will run back home to deliver a glowing report about you to Lady Natalie." Lillian paused and gave him a mock-threatening glance. "Aren't you?"

Rafe smiled at his sister while he dandled her eight-month-old infant Merritt on his knee. The baby was dark-haired and brown-eyed like both her parents, with rosy cheeks and grasping little hands. After tugging off one of his waistcoat buttons with a determined yank, the baby attempted to put it in her mouth. "No, darling," Rafe said, prying the button out of the wet clenched fist, and Merritt began to howl in protest. "I'm sorry," he said contritely. "I'd scream too if someone took away something I fancied. But you might choke on that, love, and then your mother would have me shanghaied to China."

"That's only if Westcliff didn't reach you first," Lillian said, taking the squalling baby from him. "There, darling. Mommy won't let mean old Uncle Rafe bother you any longer." She grinned and wrinkled her nose impishly at him as she soothed her daughter.

Marriage and motherhood became Lillian, Rafe thought. His sister had always been a headstrong creature, but now she seemed calmer and happier than he had ever seen her before. He could only credit Westcliff for that, although how such a proper and autocratic man could accomplish such a change in Lillian was a mystery. One would have thought the pair would have killed each other within the first month of marriage.

After the baby had quieted and Lillian had given her to a nurserymaid to take upstairs, Annabelle and Evie arrived.

Rising to his feet, Rafe bowed to the ladies as introductions were made.

Mrs. Annabelle Hunt, wife to the railroad entrepreneur Simon Hunt, was said to be one of the great beauties of England. It was difficult to imagine that any woman could eclipse her. She was the perfect English Rose, with honey-blond hair and blue eyes, and a pure, fair complexion. Not only would her figure have driven a saint to sin but her expression was so lively and beguiling that it instantly put him at ease.

Evie, Lady St. Vincent, was not nearly so approachable. However, Lillian had already warned Rafe that Evie's shyness was often mistaken for reserve. She was unconventionally lovely, her skin lightly freckled, her hair rampantly red. Her blue eyes contained a cautious friendliness and vulnerability that touched Rafe.

"My dear Mr. Bowman," Annabelle said with an engaging laugh, "I should have known you anywhere, even without an introduction. You and Lillian share a distinct resemblance. Are all the Bowmans so tall and dark-haired?"

"All except Daisy," Rafe replied. "I'm afraid the first four of us took up so much height, there was nothing left for her when she arrived."

"What Daisy lacks in height," Lillian said, "she makes up for in personality."

Rafe laughed. "True. I want to see the little scamp, and hear from her own lips that she married Matthew

Swift willingly, and not because Father bludgeoned her into it."

"Daisy truly l-loves Mr. Swift," Evie said earnestly.

At the sound of her stammer, which was something else Lillian had warned him about, Rafe gave her a reassuring smile. "I'm glad to hear it," he said gently. "I've always thought Swift was a decent fellow."

"It never bothered you, the way Father adopted him as a *de facto* son?" Lillian asked acerbically, seating herself and gesturing for the others to do the same.

"Just the opposite," Rafe said. "I was glad of anyone or anything that took Father's attention away from me. I've had enough of the old man's damned short fuse for a lifetime. The only reason I'm willing to put up with it now is because I want joint proprietorship of the company's European expansion."

Annabelle looked bemused at their frankness. "It appears we're not bothering with discretion today."

Rafe grinned. "I doubt there is much about the Bowmans that Lillian hasn't already told you. So by all means, let's dispense with discretion and move on to the interesting subjects."

"Are the ladies of London a subject of interest?" Lillian asked.

"Definitely. Tell me about them."

"They're different here than in New York," Lillian warned him. "Especially the younger ones. When you are introduced to a proper English girl, she will keep her gaze fixed on the ground, and she won't chatter and gush on as we Americans do. English girls are far more sheltered, and not at all used to the company of men.

So don't even think about discussing business or political affairs, or anything of the sort."

"What am I allowed to talk about?" Rafe asked apprehensively.

"Music, art, and horses," Annabelle said. "And remember that English girls seldom offer their views on anything, but instead prefer to repeat their parents' opinions."

"But after they are m-married," Evie said, "they will be far more inclined to reveal their true selves."

Rafe gave her a wry glance. "How difficult would it be to find out about a girl's true self *before* I marry her?"

"Almost imp-possible," Evie said gravely, and Rafe began to smile until he realized she wasn't joking.

Now he was beginning to understand why Lillian and her friends were trying to find out more about Lady Natalie and her character. Apparently it wasn't going to come from Lady Natalie herself.

Looking from Lillian's face to those of Annabelle and Evie, Rafe said slowly, "I appreciate your help, ladies. It occurs to me that I may need it more than I thought."

"The person who will be most helpful," Lillian said, "is Miss Appleton. One hopes." She parted the lace curtains at the window to glance at the street. "And if I'm not mistaken, she has just arrived."

Rafe stood in a perfunctory manner while Miss Appleton came into the entrance hall. Lillian went to greet her while a servant collected her coat and bonnet. Rafe supposed he should be grateful to the old biddy for coming to visit, but all he could think of was how quickly they might be able to obtain the necessary information and be rid of her.

He watched without interest as she came into the parlor. She wore a dull blue gown of the practical and well-made sort seen on retainers and the higher caliber of servants.

His gaze traveled up to the neat shape of her waist, the gentle curves of her breasts, and then to her face. He felt a little stab of surprise as he saw that she was young, no more than Daisy's age. From her expression, one could deduce that she wasn't any happier to be there than Rafe. But there was a suggestion of tenderness and humor in the soft shape of her mouth, and delicate strength in the lines of her nose and chin.

Her beauty was not cool and pristine, but warm and slightly disheveled. Her brown hair, shiny as ribbons, seemed to have been pinned up in a hurry. As she removed her gloves with a neat tug at each fingertip, she glanced at Rafe with ocean-green eyes.

That look left no doubt that Miss Appleton neither liked nor trusted him. Nor should she, Rafe thought with a flash of amusement. He was not exactly known for his honorable intentions where women were concerned.

She approached him in a composed manner that annoyed Rafe for some reason. She made him want to . . . well, he wasn't certain what, but it would begin with scooping her up and tossing her onto the nearby settee.

"Miss Appleton," Lillian said, "I should like to introduce my brother, Mr. Bowman."

"Miss Appleton," Rafe murmured, extending his hand.

The young woman hesitated, her pale fingers making a slight flutter beside her skirts.

"Oh, Rafe," Lillian said hastily, "that's not done here."

"My apologies." Rafe withdrew his hand, staring into
those translucent green eyes. "The handshake is common in American parlors."

Miss Appleton gave him a speculative glance. "In
London, a simple bow is best," she said in a light, clear
voice that sent a ripple of heat down the back of his
neck. "Although at times a married lady might shake
hands, an unmarried one rarely does. It is usually regarded here as a lower-class practice, and a rather personal matter, especially when done without gloves." She
studied him for a moment, the hint of a smile curving
her lips. "However, I have no objection to beginning in
the American fashion." She extended a slender hand.
"How is it done?"

The unaccountable heat lingered on the back of Rafe's
neck and crept across his shoulders. He took her slim
hand in his much larger one, surprised by the needling
sensation in his abdomen, the shot of acute awareness.
"A firm grip," he began, "is usually considered—" He
broke off, unable to speak at all as she cautiously returned the pressure of his fingers.

"Like this?" she asked, glancing up into his face.
Her cheeks had turned pink.

"Yes." Dazedly Rafe wondered what was the matter
with him. The pressure of that small, confiding hand was
affecting him more than his last mistress's most lascivi-
ous caress.

Letting go of her, he dragged his gaze away and
struggled to moderate his breathing.

Lillian and Annabelle exchanged a perplexed glance in the charged silence.

"Well," Lillian said brightly as the tea trays were brought in, "let's become better acquainted. Shall I pour?"

Annabelle lowered herself to the settee beside Lillian, while Rafe and Miss Appleton took chairs on the other side of the low table. For the next few minutes the rituals of tea were observed. Plates of toast and crumpets were passed around.

Rafe couldn't seem to stop staring at Miss Appleton, who sat straight-backed in her chair, sipping carefully at her tea. He wanted to pull the pins from her hair and wrap it around his fingers. He wanted to tumble her to the floor. She looked so proper, so good, sitting there with her skirts precisely arranged.

She made him want to be very, very bad.

THREE

Hannah had never been so uncomfortable in her life. The man sitting next to her was a beast. He stared at her as if she were some carnival curiosity. And he had already confirmed much of what she had heard about American men. Everything about him advertised a brand of excessive masculinity that she found distasteful. The slouchy, informal way he occupied his chair made her want to kick his shins.

His New York accent, the flattened vowels and lax consonants, was foreign and annoying. However, she had to admit that the voice itself . . . a deep, polished-leather baritone, was mesmerizing. And his eyes were extraordinary, dark as pitch yet gleaming with audacious fire.

He had the sun-browned complexion of a man who spent a great deal of time out of doors, and his close-shaven jaw showed the grain of a heavy beard. He was an excessively, uncompromisingly masculine creature.

Not at all a match for Natalie in any regard. He was not appropriate for the drawing room, or the parlor, or any other civilized surroundings.

Mr. Bowman addressed her with a directness that seemed nothing short of subversive. "Tell me, Miss Appleton . . . what does a lady's companion do? And do you receive wages for it?"

Oh, he was horrid to ask such a thing! Swallowing back her indignation, Hannah replied, "It is a paid position. I do not receive wages, but rather an allowance."

He tilted his head and regarded her intently. "What's the difference?"

" 'Wages' would imply that I am a servant."

"I see. And what is it you do in return for your allowance?"

His persistence was galling. "I provide companionship and conversation," she said, "and on occasion I act as chaperone to Lady Natalie. I also do light sewing, and I do small things that make Lady Natalie's life more comfortable, such as bring her tea or go on errands."

Mockery flickered in those heathen eyes. "But you're not a servant."

Hannah gave him a cool glance. "No." She decided to turn the tables on him. "What exactly does a financial speculator do?"

"I make investments. I also watch for people who are being idiotic with their investments. And then I encourage them to go at it full-tilt, until I'm left with a profit while they're standing in a pile of smoking rubble."

"How do you sleep at night?" she asked, appalled.

Bowman flashed an insolent grin. "Very well, thank you."

"I didn't mean—"

"I know what you meant, Miss Appleton. I rest easy in the knowledge that I'm doing my victims a service."

"How?"

"I teach them a valuable lesson."

Before Hannah could reply, Annabelle broke in hastily. "Dear me, we mustn't allow the conversation to drift into business talk. I hear far too much of that at home. Miss Appleton, I have heard such lovely things about Lady Natalie. How long have you been her companion?"

"For three years," Hannah answered readily. She was slightly older than her cousin, two years to be exact, and she had watched as Natalie had blossomed into the poised and dazzling girl that she was now. "Lady Natalie is a delight. Her disposition is amiable and affectionate, and she has every grace of character one could wish for. A more intelligent and charming girl could not be found."

Bowman gave a low laugh edged with disbelief. "A paragon," he said. "Unfortunately I've heard other young women advertised in equally rapturous terms. But when you meet them, there's always a flaw."

"Some people," Hannah replied, "will insist on finding flaws in others even when there are none."

"Everyone has flaws, Miss Appleton."

He was too provoking to be endured. She met his keen, dark gaze and asked, "What are yours, Mr. Bowman?"

"Oh, I'm a scoundrel," he said cheerfully. "I take

advantage of others, I care nothing for propriety, and I have an unfortunate habit of saying exactly what I think. What are yours?" He smiled at her wide-eyed silence. "Or are you by chance as perfect as Lady Natalie?"

Hannah was struck speechless by his boldness. No man had ever spoken to her in such a manner. Another woman might have withered at the derision in his voice. But something in her would not be cowed.

"Rafe," she heard Lillian say in a warning under-tone, "I'm sure *our guest* doesn't wish to be subjected to an inquisition before we've even brought out the scones."

"No, my lady," Hannah managed to say, "it's quite all right." She stared directly at Bowman. "I am far too opinionated," she told him. "I believe that is my worst flaw. I am often impulsive. And I'm dreadful at small talk. I tend to become carried away in conversation, and I go on for far too long." She paused strategically before adding, "I also have little patience with insolent people."

A brief, tumultuous silence followed as their gazes locked. Hannah could not seem to look away from him. She felt her palms turning moist and hot, and she knew her color was high.

"Well done," he said softly. "My apologies, Miss Appleton. I did not mean to give any impression of in-solence."

But he had. He had been testing her, needling her de-liberately to see what she would do. Like a cat playing with a mouse. Hannah felt a warm sensation bristling down her spine as she stared into the heathen depths of his eyes.

"Rafe," she heard Lillian exclaim with exasperation,

"if this is an example of your parlor manners, there is much work to be done before I will allow you to meet Lady Natalie."

"Lady Natalie is quite sheltered," Hannah said. "I fear you will not get very far with her, Mr. Bowman, if you are anything less than gentlemanly."

"Point taken." Bowman gave Hannah an innocent glance. "I can behave better than this."

I doubt that, she longed to say, but bit the words back. And Bowman smiled as if he could read her thoughts.

The conversation returned to the topic of Natalie, and Hannah provided answers to such questions as her preferred flowers, her favorite books and music, her likes and dislikes. It had crossed Hannah's mind to be untruthful, to put Mr. Bowman at a disadvantage with Natalie. But it was not in her nature to lie, nor was she very good at it. And then there was Lord Blandford's request. If he truly believed it would be to Natalie's advantage to marry into the Bowman family, it was not Hannah's right to stand in the way. The Blandfords had been kind to her, and they did not deserve an ill turn.

She found it a bit peculiar that Bowman asked very little about Natalie. Instead he seemed content to let the other women question her, while he drank his tea and stared at her with a coolly assessing gaze.

Of the three women, Hannah liked Annabelle the most. She had a knack for keeping the conversation entertaining, and she was amusing and well versed in many subjects. In fact, Annabelle was an example of what Natalie might become in a few years.

Were it not for Mr. Bowman's disturbing presence, Hannah would have been sorry for teatime to end. But it was with relief that she received the news that Lord Blandford's carriage had arrived to convey her back home. She didn't think she could abide much more of Bowman's unsettling stare.

"Thank you for the lovely tea," Hannah said to Lillian, standing and smoothing her skirts. "It has been a delight to make your acquaintance."

Lillian grinned with the same flash of mischief that Bowman had displayed before. With their spicy brown eyes and gleaming sable hair, there was no doubting their family resemblance. Except that Lillian was far nicer. "You are very kind to tolerate us, Miss Appleton. I do hope we haven't behaved too badly."

"Not at all," Hannah replied. "I look forward to seeing you in Hampshire soon."

In a matter of days, Hannah would be leaving for Lillian and Lord Westcliff's country estate with Natalie and the Blandfords for an extended visit over Christmas. It would last more than a fortnight, during which time Mr. Bowman and Natalie would have ample opportunity to discover whether they suited. Or not.

"Yes, it will be a grand, glorious Christmas," Lillian exclaimed, her eyes glowing. "Music, feasting, dancing, and all kinds of fun. And Lord Westcliff has promised that we will have an absolutely *towering* Christmas tree."

Hannah smiled, caught up in her enthusiasm. "I've never seen one before."

"Haven't you? Oh, it's magical when all the candles are lit. Christmas trees are quite the fashion in New York, where I was brought up. It started as a German tradition, and it's catching on rapidly in America, though it's not common in England. Yet."

"The royal family has had Christmas trees for some time," Annabelle said. "Queen Charlotte always put one up at Windsor. And I've heard that Prince Albert has continued the tradition after the manner of his German heritage."

"I look forward to viewing the Christmas tree," Hannah said, "and spending the holiday with all of you." She bowed to the women, and paused uncertainly as she glanced up at Bowman. He was very tall, his presence so forceful and vital that she felt a shock of awareness as he moved closer to her. As she glanced up at Bowman's handsome, arrogant face, all she could think of was how much she disliked him. And yet dislike had never made her mouth go dry like this. Dislike had never sent her pulse into a swift, tripping beat, nor had it knotted in the pit of her stomach.

Hannah nodded to him in the approximation of a bow.

Bowman smiled, his teeth very white in his sunbrowned face. "You shook my hand before," he reminded her, and extended his palm.

Such audacity. She didn't want to touch him again, and he knew it. Her chest felt very tight, compressing until she was forced to take an extra breath. But at the same time she felt a wry, irrepressible smile curve her lips. He was a scoundrel indeed. Natalie would discover that soon enough.

"So I did," Hannah said, and reached out for his hand. A quiver went through her frame as she felt his fingers close around hers. It was a powerful hand, capable of crushing her delicate bones with ease, but his hold was gentle. And hot. Hannah sent him a bewildered glance and tugged free, while her heart pounded heavily. She wished he would stop staring at her—she could actually feel his gaze on her downbent head. "The carriage is waiting," she said unsteadily.

"I'll take you to the entrance hall," she heard Lillian say, "and we'll ring for your cloak and—" She broke off as she heard the sound of a crying baby. "Oh, dear."

A nurserymaid came into the parlor, holding a dark-haired infant bundled in a pink blanket. "Beg pardon, milady, but she won't stop crying."

"My daughter Merritt," Lillian explained to Hannah. Reaching out for the infant, she cuddled and soothed her. "Poor darling, you've been fretful today. Miss Appleton, if you'll wait a moment—"

"I'll see myself out," Hannah said, smiling. "Stay here with your daughter, my lady."

"I'll go with you," Bowman offered easily.

"Thank you, Rafe," came Lillian's grateful reply, before Hannah could object.

Feeling a pang of nerves in her stomach, Hannah left the parlor with Rafe Bowman. Before he reached for the bell pull, she murmured, "If you have no objection, I would like to speak with you privately for a moment."

"Of course." His gaze swept over her, his eyes containing the devilish glint of a man who was well accustomed to having private moments with women he barely knew. His fingers slid around her elbow as he drew her with him to the shadow beneath the stairs.

"Mr. Bowman," Hannah whispered with desperate earnestness, "I have neither the right nor the desire to correct your manners, but . . . this matter of the handshake . . ."

His head bent over hers. "Yes?"

"Please, you *must* not extend your hand to an older person, or to a man of greater prestige, or most of all to a lady, unless any of these people offer their hands to you first. It's simply not done here. And as vexing and annoying as you are, I still don't wish you to be slighted."

To her surprise, Bowman appeared to listen closely. When he replied, his tone was infused with quiet gravity. "That is kind of you, Miss Appleton."

She looked away from him, her gaze chasing round the floor, the walls, the underside of the stairs. Her breath came in anxious little gusts. "I'm not being kind. I just said you were vexing and annoying. You've made no effort to be polite."

"You're right," he said gently. "But believe me, I'm even more annoying when I'm trying to be polite."

They were standing too close, the crisp scents of his wool coat and starched linen shirt drifting to her nostrils. And the deeper underlying fragrance of male skin, fresh and spiced with bergamot shaving soap. Bowman watched her with the same intensity, very nearly fascination, that he had shown in the parlor. It made her nervous, being stared at in such a way.

Hannah squared her shoulders. "I must be frank, Mr. Bowman. I do not believe that you and Lady Natalie will suit in any way. There is not one atom of likeness between you. No common ground. I think it would be a disaster. And it is my duty to share this opinion with Lady Natalie. In fact, I will do whatever is necessary to stand in the way of your betrothal. And though you may not believe this, it is for your own good as well as Lady Natalie's."

Bowman didn't seem at all concerned by her opinion, or her warning. "There's nothing I can do to change your opinion of me?"

"No, I'm quite stubborn in my opinions."

"Then I'll have to show you what happens to women who stand in my way."

His hands slipped around her with an easy stealth that caught her completely unaware. Before she comprehended what was happening, one powerful arm had brought her against the animal heat of his hard masculine body. With his other hand, he grasped the nape of her neck, and tilted her head backward. And his mouth took hers.

Hannah went rigid in his arms, straining backward, but he followed and secured her more firmly against him. He let her feel how much bigger he was, how much stronger, and as she gasped and tried to speak, he took swift advantage of her parted lips.

A wild jolt went through her, and she reached up to push his head away. His mouth was experienced and unexpectedly soft, possessing hers with seductive skill. She had never thought a kiss could have a taste, an intimate flavor. She had never dreamed that her body would welcome something her mind utterly rejected.

But as Bowman forced her to accept the deep, drugging kiss, she felt herself going limp, her senses overrun. Her traitorous fingers curled into the thick raven locks of his hair, the strands as heavy as raw silk. And instead of rebuffing him, she found herself holding him closer. Her mouth trembled and opened beneath his expert persuasion as liquid fire raced through her veins.

Slowly Bowman took his lips from hers and guided her head to his chest, which moved beneath her cheek with strong, uneven breaths. A mischievous whisper tickled her ear. "This is how we court girls in America. We grab them and kiss them. And if they don't like it, we do it again, harder and longer, until they surrender. It saves us hours of witty repartee."

Looking up at him sharply, Hannah saw a dance of laughter in his wicked dark eyes, and she drew in a breath of outrage. "I'm going to tell—"

"Tell anyone you like. I'll deny it."

Her brows pulled together in a scowl. "You are worse than a scoundrel. You're a *cad*."

"If you didn't like it," he murmured, "you shouldn't have kissed me back."

"I did *not*—"

His mouth crushed over hers again. She made a choked sound, hitting his chest with her fist. But he was impervious to the blow, his hand coming up and engulfing her entire fist. And he consumed her with a deeply voluptuous kiss, stroking inside her, doing things she had never suspected people did while kissing. She was shocked by the searing invasion, and even more by the pleasure it gave her, all her senses opening to receive more. She wanted him to stop, but more than that, she wanted him to go on forever.

Hannah felt his breath rush fast and hot against her cheek, his chest rising and falling with unsteady force. He let go of her hand, and she leaned weakly against him, gripping his shoulders for balance. The urgent pressure of his mouth forced her head back. She surrendered with a soft moan, needing something she had no name for, some way to soothe the anxious rhythm of her pulse. It seemed that if she could just pull him closer, tighter, it might ease the sensual agitation that filled every part of her.

Drawing back reluctantly, Bowman finished the kiss with a teasing nudge of his lips, and cradled the side of her face in his hand. The amusement had faded from his eyes, replaced by a dangerous smolder.

"What is your first name?" His whisper fanned like a waft of steam across her lips. At her silence, he dragged his mouth lightly over hers. "Tell me, or I'll kiss you again."

"Hannah," she said faintly, knowing she could not bear any more.

His thumb caressed the scarlet surface of her cheek. "From now on, Hannah, no matter what you say or do, I'm going to look at your mouth and remember how sweet you taste." A self-mocking smile curved his lips as he added quietly, "Damn it."

Releasing her with care, he went to the bell pull and rang for a housemaid. When Hannah's cloak and hat were brought, he took them from the maid. "Come, Miss Appleton."

Hannah couldn't bring herself to look at him. She knew her face was terribly red. Without doubt, she had never been so mortified and confused in her life. She waited in dazed silence as he deftly draped the cloak around her and fastened it at her throat.

"Until we meet again in Hampshire," she heard him

say. The tip of his forefinger touched her chin. "Look up, sweetheart."

Hannah obeyed jerkily. He placed the hat on her head, carefully adjusting the brim. "Did I frighten you?" he whispered.

Glaring at him, she lifted her chin another notch. Her voice shook only a little. "I am sorry to disappoint you, Mr. Bowman. But I am neither frightened *nor* intimidated."

A gleam of humor flickered in those obsidian eyes. "I should warn you, Hannah: when we meet at Stony Cross Park, take care to avoid the mistletoe. For both our sakes."

After the delectable Miss Appleton had departed, Rafe remained in the entrance hall, lowering himself to a heavy oak bench. Aroused and bemused, he pondered his unexpected loss of control. He had only meant to give the young woman a peck, just enough to fluster and disconcert her. But the kiss had flared into something so urgent, so fiercely pleasurable, that he hadn't been able to stop himself from taking far more than he should have.

He would have liked to kiss that innocent mouth for hours. He wanted to demolish every one of her inhibitions until she was wrapped around him, naked and crying for him to take her. Thinking of how difficult it would be to seduce her, and how much damned fun it would be to get under her skirts, he felt himself turning uncomfortably hard. A slow, wry smile crossed his face as he reflected that if *this* was what he could expect from Englishwomen, he was going to take up permanent residence in London.

Hearing footsteps, Rafe lifted his gaze. Lillian had come into the entrance hall. She regarded him with fond exasperation.

"How's the baby?" Rafe asked.

"Annabelle's holding her. Why are you still out here?"

"I needed a moment to cool my . . . temper."

Folding her slender arms across her chest, Lillian shook her head slowly. She was beautiful in a bold, clean-featured way, as spirited and raffish as a female pirate. She and Rafe had always understood each other, perhaps because neither of them had been able to tolerate the stringent rules set by their parents.

"Only you," Lillian said without heat, "could turn a respectable teatime visit into a sparring match."

Rafe grinned without remorse and glanced at the front door reflectively. "Something about her brings out the devil in me."

"Well, you had better contain it, dear. Because if you wish to win Lady Natalie, you'll have to display far more courtesy and polish than you did in that parlor. What do you think Miss Appleton is going to tell her employers about you?"

"That I'm an unprincipled, ill-mannered villain?" Rafe shrugged and said in a reasonable manner, "But they already know I'm from Wall Street."

Lillian's gingerbread-colored eyes narrowed as she regarded him speculatively. "Since you don't seem at all concerned, I'll have to assume that you know what you're doing. But let me remind you that Lady Natalie wants to marry a gentleman."

"In my experience," Rafe said lazily, "nothing makes

women complain nearly so much as getting what they want."

Lillian chuckled. "Oh, this should be an interesting holiday. Will you come back to the parlor?"

"In a moment. Still cooling."

She gave him a quizzical glance. "Your temper takes a long time to subside, doesn't it?"

"You have no idea," he told her gravely.

Going back into the parlor, Lillian stood in the doorway and regarded her friends. Annabelle sat with Merritt resting placidly in her arms, while Evie was pouring a last cup of tea.

"What did he say?" Annabelle asked.

Lillian rolled her eyes. "My idiot brother doesn't seem the least bit worried that Miss Appleton is sure to deliver a scathing report about him to the Blandfords and Lady Natalie." She sighed. "That didn't go at all well, did it? Have you *ever* seen such instant animosity between two people for no apparent reason?"

"Yes," Evie replied.

"I believe so," Annabelle said.

Lillian frowned. "When? Who?" she demanded, and was mystified when they smiled at each other.

FOUR

To Hannah's astonishment, Natalie was not only *not* shocked by her account of the visit with Rafe Bowman, she was highly entertained. By the time Hannah had finished the account of the kiss beneath the stairs, Natalie had collapsed on the bed in a fit of giggles.

"Natalie," Hannah said, frowning, "clearly I haven't managed to convey how dreadful that man was. *Is.* He's a barbarian. A brute. A *clod.*"

"Apparently so." Still chortling, Natalie sat up. "I look forward to meeting him."

"What?"

"He's quite manipulative, our Mr. Bowman. He knew you would tell me what he had done, and that I would be intrigued. And when I see him in Hampshire, he'll act the perfect gentleman in the hopes of setting me off balance."

"You shouldn't be intrigued, you should be appalled!"

Natalie smiled and patted her hand. "Oh, Hannah, you don't know how to manage men. You mustn't take everything so seriously."

"But courtship is a serious matter," Hannah protested. It was at moments like this that she understood the differences between herself and her younger cousin. Natalie seemed to have a more thorough understanding of social maneuvering, of the process of pursuit and capture, than Hannah ever would.

"Oh, heavens, the moment a girl approaches courtship as a serious matter is the moment she's lost the game. We must guard our hearts and hide our feelings carefully, Hannah. It's the only way to win."

"I thought courtship was a process of revealing one's heart," Hannah said. "Not winning a game."

Natalie smiled. "I don't know where you get such ideas. If you want to bring a man up to scratch, never reveal your heart to him. At least not early on. Men only value something when they have to put some effort into getting it." She tapped her forefinger on her chin. "Hmmn . . . I shall have to come up with a good counter-strategy."

Climbing off the bed, Hannah went to retrieve some gloves and stockings and other items that had been dropped carelessly to the floor. She had never minded tidying up after Natalie. Hannah had met other lady's companions whose charges had made their lives a misery, treating them with contempt and subjecting them to all kinds of small cruelties. Natalie, on the other hand, was kind and affectionate, and although she could be a trifle self-absorbed on occasion, it was nothing that time and maturity wouldn't cure.

Placing the personal articles in a dresser drawer, Hannah turned to face Natalie, who was still ruminating.

Natalie was a pretty sight, tumbled on the white ruffled bed, her hair falling in golden curls. Her blue-eyed sunny appeal had stolen many a gentleman's heart during her first season. And her delicately regretful rejections of her suitors had done nothing to dampen their ardor. Long after the season had ended, towering arrangements of flowers were delivered to the Blandford mansion, and calling cards piled up on the silver tray in the entrance hall.

Absently Natalie wound a lock of shimmering hair around her finger. "Mr. Bowman is betting on the fact that since I went through an entire season without settling on someone, I must have tired of all these bland, respectable lords of leisure. And since it's been months since the season ended, he also assumes that I am bored and eager for a challenge." She gave an abbreviated laugh. "He is correct on all counts."

"The proper way for him to get your attention is not to ravish your companion," Hannah muttered.

"You weren't ravished, you were kissed." Natalie's eyes twinkled mischievously as she asked, "Now confess, Hannah—does he kiss nicely?"

Remembering the warm erotic sensation of Bowman's mouth, Hannah felt the damnable color sweep over her again. "I don't know," she said shortly. "I have no basis for comparison."

Natalie's eyes widened. "You mean you've never been kissed before?"

Hannah shook her head.

"But surely Mr. Clark—"

"No." Hannah raised her fingers to her hot cheeks.

"He must have tried," Natalie insisted. "You've spent so much time in his company."

"I've been working for him," Hannah protested. "Helping with his manuscript and papers."

"You mean you've actually been taking dictation from him?"

Hannah gave her a bewildered glance. "What else would I have been doing?"

"I always assumed when you said you'd been 'taking dictation' from him that you were letting him kiss you."

Hannah's mouth fell open. "When I said I'd been 'taking dictation,' I meant that I had been taking dictation!"

Natalie was clearly disappointed. "My goodness. If you have spent *that* much time with him, and he has never once kissed you, I'd say that is proof of the fact that his passion for his work will eclipse all else. Even a wife. We must find someone else for you."

"I wouldn't mind taking second place to Mr. Clark's work," Hannah said earnestly. "He will be a great man someday. He will do so much good for others—"

"Great men don't necessarily make good husbands. And you're too dear and lovely to be wasted on him." Natalie shook her head in disgust. "Why, any of my leftovers from last season would be better for you than silly old Mr. Clark."

A troubling thought occurred to Hannah, but she was almost afraid to voice her suspicion. "Natalie, did you ever let one of your suitors kiss you?"

"No," Natalie said reassuringly.

Hannah let out a sigh of relief.

"I let nearly all of them kiss me," Natalie continued cheerfully. "On separate occasions, of course."

Aghast, Hannah leaned hard against the dresser. "But . . . but I was watching over you . . ."

"You're a terrible chaperone, Hannah. You often become so absorbed in conversation that you forget to keep an eye on me. It's one of the reasons I adore you so."

Hannah had never dreamed that her pretty, high-spirited cousin would have let any young man presume so far. Much less *several*. "You know you should never allow such liberties," she said weakly. "It will cause rumors, and you might be labeled as fast, and then . . ."

"No one will enter an engagement with me?" Natalie smiled wryly. "Last season I received four proposals of marriage, and had I cared to encourage any more, I could have gotten another half dozen. Believe me, Hannah, I know how to manage men. Bring my hairbrush, please."

Obeying, Hannah had to acknowledge that there was good reason for Natalie to be so self-assured. She was, or would be, the ideal bride for any man. She gave the silver-backed brush to Natalie and watched her draw it through a flurry of rich blond curls. "Natalie, why didn't you accept any of those offers last season?"

"I'm waiting for someone special," came the thoughtful reply. "I should hate to settle for anyone ordinary." Natalie smiled as she added flippantly, "When I kiss a man, I want to hear the angels sing."

"What about Lord Travers?" Of all the gentlemen

who had shown an interest in Natalie, the one Hannah had the highest regard for was Edward, Lord Travers. He was a sober, quiet gentleman, careful in appearance and bearing. Although his countenance did not lend itself to outright handsomeness, his features were strong and regular. He did not seem dazzled by Natalie, and yet he paid a close and respectful attention to her whenever she was present. And he was rich and titled, which, along with his other qualities, made him an excellent catch.

The mention of Travers drew a frown from Natalie. "He is the only man of my acquaintance who will not make an advance to me, even when handed a perfectly good opportunity. I chalk it up to his age."

Hannah couldn't help laughing. "His age?"

"He is on the wrong side of thirty, after all."

"He is mature," Hannah allowed. "But he is also confident, intelligent, and from all appearances, in full vigor."

"Then why hasn't he kissed me?"

"Because he respects you?" Hannah suggested.

"I would rather be regarded with passion than respect."

"Well, then," Hannah said wryly, "I would say that Mr. Bowman is your man."

The mention of Bowman restored Natalie's good spirits. "Possibly so. Now, Hannah, tell Mama and Papa that Mr. Bowman was exquisitely well behaved. No, they won't believe that, he's American. Tell them he was quite presentable. And not one mention of the kiss under the stairs."

FIVE

Hampshire
Stony Cross Park

Hannah had never expected to have the opportunity to see Stony Cross Park. Invitations to Lord Westcliff's famed country estate were not easy to obtain. Located in the southern county of Hampshire, Stony Cross Park was reputed to have some of the finest acreage in England. The variety of flowering fields, fertile wet meadows, bogs and ancient forests made it a beautiful and sought-after place to visit. Generations of the same families had been invited to the same annual events and parties. To be excluded from the guest list would have resulted in the most inconsolable outrage.

"And just think," Natalie had mused on the long carriage ride from London. "If I marry Lord Westcliff's brother-in-law, I will be able to visit Stony Cross Park any time I wish!"

"All for the price of having Mr. Bowman as your husband," Hannah said dryly. Although she had not told Lord and Lady Blandford about the stolen kiss, she had made it clear that she did not believe Bowman would be a suitable partner for Natalie. The Blandfords, however, had counseled her to reserve judgment until they all became better acquainted with him.

Lady Blandford, as blond and lovely and ebullient as her daughter, caught her breath as Stony Cross Manor loomed in the distance. The house was European in design, built of honey-colored stone with four graceful towers so tall they seemed about to pierce holes in the early evening sky, which was washed with an orange and lavender sunset.

Set on a bluff by the Itchen River, Stony Cross Manor was fantastically landscaped with gardens and orchards, riding courses, and magnificent walking paths that led through massive tracts of forest and parkland. Owing to Hampshire's felicitous southern location, the climate was milder than the rest of England.

"Oh, Natalie," Lady Blandford exclaimed, "to think of being affiliated with such a family! And as a Bowman, you could have your own country manor, and a London house, and a villa on the Continent, not to mention your own carriage and team of four, and the most beautiful gowns and jewels . . ."

"Heavens, are the Bowmans *that* rich?" Natalie asked with a touch of surprise. "And will Mr. Bowman inherit the majority of the family business?"

"A handsome portion of it, to be sure," Lord Blandford replied, smiling at his daughter's bright-eyed interest. "He has his own wealth, and the promise of much more to come. Mr. Bowman the elder has indicated that upon your betrothal to his son, there will be rich rewards for both of you."

"I should think so," Natalie said pragmatically, "since it would be a comedown for me to marry a commoner when I could just as easily have a peer." There was no disparagement or arrogance intended in her statement. It was a fact that some doors would be open to a peer's wife that would never be open to the wife of an American manufacturer.

As the carriage stopped before the manor entrance, Hannah noticed that the estate was laid out in the French manner, with the stables located at the front of the house instead of being concealed to the side or behind it. The stables were housed in a building with huge arched doorways, forming one side of a stone-flagged entrance courtyard.

Footmen helped them from the carriage, and Westcliff's stablemen came to help with the horses. More servants hurried to collect the trunks and valises. An elderly butler admitted them into the massive entrance hall, where regiments were going back and forth; housemaids with baskets of linens, footmen with crates and boxes, and others engaged in cleaning, polishing, and sweeping.

"Lord and Lady Blandford!" Lillian came to them, looking radiant in a dark red gown, her sable hair neatly confined in a snood made of jeweled netting. With her brilliant smile and relaxed friendliness, she was so engaging that Hannah understood why the famously dignified earl of Westcliff had married her. Lillian bowed to them, and they responded in kind.

"Welcome to Stony Cross Park," Lillian said. "I hope your journey was comfortable? Please excuse the clamor and bustle, we're desperately trying to prepare for the hordes of guests who will pour in tomorrow. After you refresh yourselves, you must come to the main parlor. My parents are there, and of course my brother, and—" She broke off as she saw Natalie. "My dear Lady Natalie." Her voice softened. "I have so looked forward to meeting you. We will do everything possible to make certain you have a lovely holiday."

"Thank you, my lady," Natalie replied demurely. "I have no doubt it will be splendid." She smiled at Lillian. "My companion told me there will be a Christmas tree."

"Fourteen feet high," Lillian said enthusiastically. "We're having a devil of a . . . that is, a most difficult time decorating it, as the top branches are impossible to reach. But we have extending ladders and many tall footmen, so we will prevail." She turned to Hannah. "Miss Appleton. A pleasure to see you again."

"Thank you, my—" Hannah paused as she realized that Lillian had extended her hand. Bemusedly Hannah reached out to take it, and gave her a quizzical glance.

The countess winked at her, and Hannah realized she was being teased. She burst out laughing at the private joke, and returned the warm pressure of Lillian's fingers.

"In light of your remarkable tolerance for the Bowmans," Lillian told her, "you must come to the parlor, too."

"Yes, my lady."

The housekeeper came to show them to their rooms, leading them across what seemed to be miles of flooring.

"Hannah, why did Lady Westcliff shake your hand?"

Natalie whispered. "And why did you both seem to find it so amusing?"

Natalie and Hannah were to share a room, with Natalie occupying the main bed and Hannah sleeping in a cozy antechamber. The room was beautifully appointed with flowered paper on the walls and mahogany furniture, and a bed with a lace canopy.

While Natalie washed her hands and face, Hannah found a clean day dress for her and shook it out. The dress was a becoming shade of blue, with a dropped shoulder line filled in with lace, and long slim-fitting sleeves. Smiling in anticipation of meeting the Bowmans, Natalie sat before the vanity mirror while Hannah brushed and repinned her coiffure. After making certain that Natalie's appearance was perfect, her nose lightly dusted with powder, her lips smoothed with rosewater salve, Hannah went to her own valise and began to rummage through it.

Lady Blandford appeared in the doorway, looking refreshed and poised. "Come, girls," she said serenely. "It is time for us to join the company downstairs."

"A few more minutes, Mama," Natalie said. "Hannah hasn't yet changed her dress or tidied her hair."

"We mustn't keep everyone waiting," Lady Blandford insisted. "Come as you are, Hannah. No one will notice."

"Yes, ma'am," Hannah said obediently, concealing a pang of dismay. Her traveling clothes were dusty, and her hair was threatening to fall from its pins. She did not want to face the Bowmans and the Westcliffs in this condition. "I would prefer to stay up here and help the maids to unpack the trunks—"

"No," Lady Blandford said with an impatient sigh. "Ordinarily I would agree, but the countess requested your presence. You must come as you are, Hannah, and try to be unassuming."

"Yes, ma'am." Hannah pushed the straggles of loose hair back from her face and dashed to the washstand to splash her face. Water spots made little dark patches on her traveling gown. Groaning inwardly, she followed Natalie and Lady Blandford from the room.

"I'm sorry," Natalie whispered to her, frowning. "We shouldn't have taken so much time getting *me* ready."

"Nonsense," Hannah murmured, reaching out to pat her arm. "You're the one everyone wants to see. Lady Blandford is right—no one will notice me."

The house was beautifully ornamented, the windows swathed in gold silk edged with dangling gold tinsel balls, the doorways surmounted by swags of beribboned evergreens and holly and ivy. Tables were loaded with candles and arrangements of everlasting flowers such as chrysanthemums and Christmas roses and camellias. And someone, slyly, had adorned several doorways with kissing balls hung with evergreen ropes.

Glancing at the bunches of mistletoe, Hannah felt a stab of nervousness as she thought of Rafe Bowman. *Calm yourself,* she thought with a self-deprecating grin, glancing down at her disheveled dress. *He certainly won't try to kiss you now, not even beneath a cartload of mistletoe.*

They entered the main parlor, a large and comfortably furnished room with a game table, and piles of books and periodicals, a pianoforte, a standing sewing hoop, and a small secretary desk.

The first person Hannah noticed was Marcus, Lord Westcliff, a man with an imposing and powerful presence that was unusual for a man still only in his thirties. As he stood to meet them, Hannah saw that the earl was only of medium height, but he was superbly fit and self-assured. Westcliff carried himself with the ease of a man who was entirely comfortable with his own authority.

While Lillian made the introductions, Hannah shrank back into the corner of the room, observing the scene. She stared discreetly at the Bowmans as they met the Blandfords.

Thomas Bowman was stout, short, and ruddy, his mouth overhung with a large walruslike mustache. And his shining head was adorned with a toupee that seemed ready to jump off his scalp and flee the room.

His wife, Mercedes, on the other hand, was whippet-thin and brittle, with hard eyes and a smile that fractured her face like cracks in a frozen pond. The only thing the pair seemed to have in common was a sense of dissatisfaction with life and each other, as if it were a blanket they both huddled under.

The Bowman children resembled each other far more than either parent, both of them tall and irreverent and relaxed. It seemed they had been formed by some magical combination of just the right features from both parents.

Hannah watched covertly as Lillian introduced Rafe Bowman to Natalie. She could not see Natalie's expression, but she had an excellent view of Bowman. His strapping form was clad in a perfectly fitted dark coat and gray trousers, and a crisp white shirt with a neatly knotted black cravat. He bowed to Natalie and murmured something that elicited a breathless laugh. There was no denying it—with his unvarnished masculinity and bold dark eyes, Rafe Bowman was, to put it in a popular slang term, a stunner.

Hannah wondered what he thought of her cousin. Bowman's face was unreadable, but she was certain that he could find no fault with Natalie.

As everyone in the room made small talk, Hannah inched toward the door. If at all possible, she was going to slip from the room unnoticed. The open threshold beckoned invitingly, promising freedom. Oh, it would be lovely to escape to her room, and change into clean clothes and brush out her hair in privacy. But just as she reached the doorway, she heard Rafe Bowman's deep voice.

"Miss Appleton. Surely you won't deprive us of your charming company."

Hannah stopped abruptly and turned to find the collective gaze on her, just at the moment she least wanted attention. She longed to glare at Bowman. No, she longed to *kill* him. Instead, she adopted a neutral expression and murmured, "Good afternoon, Mr. Bowman."

Lillian called to her immediately. "Miss Appleton, do come forward. I want to introduce you to my husband."

Repressing a heavy sigh, Hannah pushed back the locks that dangled over her face and came forward.

"Westcliff," Lillian said to her husband. "This is Lady Natalie's companion, Miss Hannah Appleton."

Hannah bowed and glanced apprehensively at the earl. His features were dark and austere, perhaps a bit forbidding. But as his gaze rested on her face, she saw that his eyes were kind. He spoke in a gravel-in-velvet voice that fell pleasantly on her ears. "Welcome, Miss Appleton."

"Thank you, my lord," she said. "And many thanks for allowing me to spend the holiday here."

"The countess enjoyed your company at tea last week," Westcliff replied, smiling briefly at Lillian. "Anyone who pleases her also pleases me." The smile transformed him, warming his face.

Lillian spoke to her husband with breezy casualness, as if he were a mere mortal man instead of England's most distinguished peer. "Westcliff, I think you will want to talk to Miss Appleton about her work with Mr. Samuel Clark." She glanced at Hannah as she added, "The earl has read some of his writings, and quite enjoyed them."

"Oh, I do not work *with* Mr. Clark," Hannah said hastily, "but rather *for* him, in a secretarial capacity." She gave the earl a cautious smile. "I am a bit surprised that you would have read anything by Mr. Clark, my lord."

"I am acquainted with many progressive theorists of London," Westcliff said. "What is Mr. Clark working on now?"

"Currently he is writing a speculative book on what natural laws might govern the development of the human mind."

"I would like to hear more about that during supper."

"Yes, my lord."

Lillian proceeded to introduce Hannah to her parents, who responded with pleasant nods. It was clear, however, that they had already dismissed Hannah as a person of no consequence.

"Rafe," the countess suggested to her brother, "perhaps you might take Lady Blandford and Lady Natalie on a walk round the house before supper."

"Oh, yes," Natalie said at once. "May we, Mama?"

"That sounds lovely," Lady Blandford said.

Bowman smiled at them both. "It would be my pleasure." He turned to Hannah. "Will you come also, Miss Appleton?"

"*No,*" she said quickly, and then realized her refusal had been a shade too forceful. She softened her tone. "I will tour the manor later, thank you."

His gaze swept over her and returned to her face. "My services may not be available then."

She stiffened at the feather-soft jeer in his voice, but she couldn't seem to break their shared gaze. In the warm parlor light, his eyes held glints of gold and cinnamon-brown. "Then somehow I will have to make do without you, Mr. Bowman," she replied tartly, and he grinned.

"You didn't tell me that Mr. Bowman was so handsome," Natalie said after supper. The hour was late, and the long journey from London, followed by a lengthy repast, had left both girls exhausted. They had retired to their room while the company downstairs lingered over tea and port.

Although the menu had been exquisite, featuring dishes such as roasted capon stuffed with truffles, and herb-crusted standing ribs of beef, supper had been an uncomfortable affair for Hannah. She was well aware of her own disheveled appearance, having found barely enough time to wash and change into a fresh gown before she'd had to dash to the dining hall. To her dismay, Lord Westcliff had persisted in asking her questions about Samuel Clark's work, which had drawn more unwanted attention to her. And all the while Rafe Bowman had kept glancing at her with a kind of audacious, unsettling interest that she could only interpret as mockery.

Forcing her thoughts back to the present, Hannah watched as Natalie sat before the vanity and pulled the combs and pins from her hair. "I suppose Mr. Bowman could be considered attractive," Hannah said reluctantly. "If one likes that sort of man."

"You mean the tall, dark-haired, dazzling sort?"

"He's not *dazzling*," Hannah protested.

Natalie laughed. "Mr. Bowman is one of the most splendidly formed men I have ever encountered. What flaw could you possibly find in his appearance?"

"His posture," Hannah muttered.

"What about it?"

"He slouches."

"He's an American. They all slouch. The weight of their wallets drags them over."

Hannah couldn't prevent a laugh. "Natalie, are you more attracted by the man himself or the size of his wallet?"

"He has many personal attractions, to be sure. A full head of hair . . . those lovely dark eyes . . . not to mention the impressive physique." Natalie picked up a brush and drew it slowly through her hair. "But I wouldn't want him if he was poor."

"Is there any man you would want if he was poor?" Hannah asked.

"Well, if I *had* to be poor, I'd rather be married to a peer. That's far better than being a nobody."

"I doubt Mr. Bowman will ever be poor," Hannah said. "He seems to have acquitted himself quite well in his financial dealings. He is a successful man, though I fear not an honorable one."

"Oh, he's a rascal, to be sure," Natalie agreed with a light laugh.

Tensing, Hannah met her cousin's gaze in the mirror. "Why do you say that? Has he said or done anything inappropriate?"

"No, and I don't expect him to, with the betrothal still on the table. But he has a sort of perpetual irreverence . . . one wonders if he could ever be sincere about anything at all."

"Perhaps it's a façade," Hannah suggested without conviction. "Perhaps he's a different man inside."

"Most people don't have façades," Natalie said dryly. "Oh, everyone thinks they do, but when you dig past the façade, there's only more façade."

"Some people are genuine."

"And *those* people are the dullest ones of all."

"*I'm* genuine," Hannah protested.

"Yes. You'll have to work on that, dear. When you're genuine, there's no mystery. And above all men like mystery in a woman."

Hannah smiled and shook her head. "Duly noted.

I'm off to bed now." After changing into a white ruffled nightgown, she went into the little antechamber and crawled into the clean soft bed. After a moment, she heard Natalie murmur, "Good night, dear," and the lamp was extinguished.

Tucking one arm beneath her pillow, Hannah lay on her side and pondered Natalie's words.

There was no doubt that Natalie was right—Hannah had nothing close to an air of mystery.

She also had no noble blood, no dowry, no great beauty, no skill or abilities that might distinguish her. And aside from the Blandfords, she had no notable connections. But she had a warm heart and a good mind, and decent looks. And she had dreams, attainable ones, of having a home and family of her own someday.

It had not escaped Hannah that in Natalie's privileged world, people expected to find happiness and love outside of marriage. But her fondest wish for Natalie was that she would end up with a husband with whom she could share some likeness of mind and heart.

And at this point, it was still highly questionable as to whether Rafe Bowman even had a heart.

SIX

While Westcliff shared cigars with Lord Blandford, Rafe went with his father to have a private conversation. They proceeded to the library, a large and handsome room that was two stories high, with mahogany bookshelves housing over ten thousand volumes. A sideboard had been built into a niche to make it flush with the bookshelves.

Rafe was thankful to see that a collection of bottles and decanters had been arranged on the sideboard's marble top. Feeling the need for something stronger than port, he found the whisky decanter. "A double?" he suggested to his father, who nodded and grunted in assent.

Rafe had always hated talking with his father. Thomas Bowman was the kind of man who determined other people's minds for them, believing that he knew them better than they knew themselves. Since early childhood Rafe had endured being told what his thoughts and motivations were, and then being punished for them. It hardly seemed to matter whether he had done something good or bad. It had only mattered what light his father had decided to cast his actions in.

And always, Thomas had held the threat of disinheritance over his head. Finally Rafe had told him to cut him off entirely and be damned. And he had gone out to make his own fortune, starting with practically nothing.

Now when he met with his father, it was on his own terms. Oh, Rafe wanted the European proprietorship of Bowman's, but he wasn't going to sell his soul for it.

He handed a whisky to his father and took a swallow, letting the creamy, sweet flavor of ester roll over his tongue.

Thomas went to sit in a leather chair before the fire. Frowning, he reached up to check the position of the toupee on his head. It had been slipping all evening.

"You might tie a chin strap on it," Rafe suggested innocently, earning a ferocious scowl.

"Your mother finds it attractive."

"Father, I find it difficult to believe that hairpiece would attract anything other than an amorous squirrel." Rafe plucked the toupee off and dropped it onto a nearby table. "Leave it off and be comfortable, for God's sake."

Thomas grumbled but didn't argue, relaxing in his chair.

Leaning an arm against the mantel, Rafe regarded his father with a faint smile.

"Well?" Thomas demanded, his heavy brows lifting expectantly. "What is your reaction to Lady Natalie?"

Rafe hitched up his shoulders in a lazy shrug. "She'll do."

The brows rushed downward. " 'She'll do'? That's all you can say?"

"Lady Natalie is no more and no less than what I expected." After taking another swallow of whisky, Rafe said flatly, "I suppose I wouldn't mind marrying her. Although she doesn't interest me in the least."

"A wife is not supposed to be interesting."

Ruefully Rafe wondered if there wasn't some hidden wisdom in that. With a wife like Lady Natalie, there would be no surprises. It would be a calm, frictionless marriage, leaving him ample time for his work and his personal pursuits. All he would have to do would be to supply her with generous bank drafts, and she would manage the household and produce children.

Lady Natalie was pleasant and beautiful, her hair blond and sleek, her manner remarkably self-assured. If Rafe ever took her to New York, she would acquit herself splendidly with the Knickerbocker crowd. Her poise, breeding, and confidence would make her much admired.

An hour in her company, and one knew virtually everything there was to know about her.

Whereas Hannah Appleton was fresh and fascinating, and at supper he hadn't been able to take his gaze off her. She did not possess Natalie's meticulously manicured beauty. Instead, there was a haphazard, cheerful bloom about her, like a fistful of wildflowers. Her hair, springing in little locks around her face, drove him mad with the urge to reach out and play with the shiny loose strands. She had a kind of delicious vitality he had never run up against before, and he instinctively wanted to be inside it, inside her.

The feeling had intensified as Rafe had witnessed Hannah conversing earnestly with Westcliff. She had been animated and adorable as she had described Samuel Clark's work concerning the development of the human mind. In fact, she had become so absorbed in the subject that she had forgotten to eat, and then she'd glanced wistfully at her still-full soup bowl while a footman had removed it.

"You will offer for her, won't you?" his father demanded, steering his thoughts back to Lady Natalie.

Rafe stared at him without expression. "Eventually. Am I supposed to get a ring, or have you already picked one out?"

"As a matter of fact, your mother purchased one she thought would be appropriate—"

"Oh, for God's sake. Would you like to propose to her for me, and come fetch me when she's given her answer?"

"I daresay I'd do it with a damned sight more enthusiasm than you," Thomas retorted.

"I'll tell you what I would do with some enthusiasm, Father: establish a large-scale soap manufacturing industry all over the Continent. And I shouldn't have to marry Lady Natalie to do it."

"Why not? Why should you be exempt from paying a price? Why shouldn't you try to please me?"

"Why indeed?" Rafe gave him a hard look. "Maybe because I knocked my head against that particular wall for years and never made a dent."

Thomas's complexion, always prone to easy color,

turned a dull plum hue as his temper ignited. "You have been a trial to me at every stage of your life. Things always came too easily to you and your siblings—spoiled, lazy creatures all of you, who never wanted to do anything."

"Lazy?" Rafe struggled for self-control, but the word set his own temper off like a match held to a tinderbox. "Only you, Father, could have five offspring do everything short of standing on their heads to impress you, and say they weren't trying hard enough. Do you know what happens when you call a clever person stupid, or a hardworking man lazy? It makes him realize there's no damn point in trying to get your approval."

"You've always thought I owed you my approval merely because you were born a Bowman."

"I don't want it any longer," Rafe said through gritted teeth, vaguely surprised to discover that the velocity of his own temper wasn't far behind his father's. "I want—" He checked himself and tossed back the rest of his whisky, swallowing hard against the velvety burn. When the glow had faded from his throat, he gave his father a cool, steady look. "I'll marry Lady Natalie, since it doesn't matter in any case. I was always going to end up with someone like her. But you can keep your damned approval. All I want is a share of Bowman's."

In the morning the guests began to arrive, an elegant clamor of well-heeled families and their servants. Trunks, valises, and parcels were brought into the manor in an unending parade. Other families would stay at neighboring estates or at the tavern in the village, coming and going to the various events that would take place at the manor.

Once Hannah was awakened by the muffled, busy sounds beyond the room, she couldn't go back to sleep. Taking care not to wake Natalie, she rose and took care of her morning ablutions, finishing by braiding her hair and pinning it in a knot at the base of her neck. She dressed in a gray-green wool gown trimmed with kilt pleating and closed in front with gleaming black buttons. Intending to go for a walk out of doors, she donned a pair of low-heeled boots and picked up a heavy plaid shawl.

Stony Cross Manor was a labyrinth of hallways and clustered rooms. Carefully Hannah made her way through the bustling house, pausing now and again to ask directions from one of the passing servants. She eventually found the morning room, which was stuffy and crowded with people she didn't know. A large breakfast buffet had been set out, featuring fish, a flitch of fried bacon, breads, poached eggs, salads, muffins, and several varieties of cheese. She poured a cup of tea, folded a bit of bacon in some bread, and slipped past a set of French doors that led to an outside terrace. The weather was bright and dry, the chilled air fomenting her breath into white mist.

Gardens and orchards spread before her, all delicately frosted and clean. Children played across the terrace, giggling as they raced back and forth. Hannah chuckled, watching them stream across the flagstones like a gaggle of goslings. They were playing a game of blow-the-feather, which involved two teams trying to keep a feather aloft by turns.

Standing to the side, Hannah consumed her bread and tea. The children's antics grew ever wilder as they hopped and blew at the feather in noisy gusts and puffs. The feather drifted to her, descending lazily.

The little girls screamed in encouragement. "Blow, miss, blow! It's girls against boys!"

After that, there was no choice. Fighting a smile, Hannah pursed her lips and exhaled sharply, sending the feather upward in a fluttering eddy. She did her part whenever the feather drifted to her, running a few steps here and there, heeding the delighted cries of her teammates.

The feather sailed over her head, and she backed up swiftly, her face upturned. But she was startled to feel herself crashing against something behind her, not a stone wall but something hard and pliant. A man's hands closed around her arms, securing her balance.

From over her head, the man blew a puff that sent the feather halfway across the terrace.

Hooting and squealing, the children raced after it.

Hannah remained still, stunned by the collision, but even more so by the realization that she recognized the feel of Rafe Bowman. The grip of his hands, the tough-muscled length of him along her back. The clean, pungent spice of his shaving soap.

Her mouth had gone dry—probably the effects of the feather game—and she tried to moisten her inner cheeks with her tongue. "What a remarkable amount of air you are able to produce, Mr. Bowman."

Smiling, he turned her carefully to face him. He was large and dashing, standing with that relaxed looseness that bothered her so. "Good morning to you, too." He looked her over with an insolently thorough glance. "Why aren't you still abed?"

"I'm an early riser." Hannah decided to throw the audacious inquiry right back at him. "Why aren't you?"

A playful glint shone in his eyes. "There's no point in lingering in bed when I'm alone."

She glanced at their surroundings to make certain none of the children could overhear. The imps had tired of their game and were filing inside the house through doors that led to the main hall. "I suspect that is a rare occurrence, Mr. Bowman."

His bland tone disguised all sincerity. "Rare, yes. Most of the time my bed is busier than a sheepfold at spring shearing."

Hannah viewed him with patent distaste. "That doesn't speak well of the women you associate with. Or of you for being so indiscriminate."

"I'm not indiscriminate. It just so happens that I'm good at finding women who meet my high standards. And I'm even better at persuading them to come to my bed."

"And then you fleece them."

A rueful smile crossed his lips. "If you don't mind, Miss Appleton, I want to retract my sheep analogy. It's becoming disagreeable even to me. Would you like to take a morning stroll?"

She shook her head in puzzlement. "With you? . . . Why?"

"You're wearing a walking dress and boots. And I assume you want to find out what my opinion of Lady Natalie is. Keep your enemy close, and so forth."

"I already know what your opinion of Lady Natalie is."

His brows lifted. "Do you? Now I insist that we walk together. I'm always fascinated to hear my opinions."

Hannah considered him sternly. "Very well," she said. "First I'll take the teacup in, and—"

"Leave it."

"On an outside table? No, someone will have to tidy up."

"Yes. That someone is called a servant. Who, unlike you, will get a salary for it."

"That doesn't mean I should make more work for someone else."

Before she could retrieve the cup, Bowman had taken it up. "I'll take care of it."

Hannah's eyes widened as she saw him stroll nonchalantly to the stone balustrade. And she gasped as he held the teacup over the side and dropped it. A splintering crash sounded from below.

"There," he said casually. "Problem solved."

It required three attempts until Hannah could finally speak. "Why did you do that? I could easily have carried it inside!"

He seemed amused by her astonishment. "I would have thought my lack of concern for material possessions would please you."

Hannah stared at him as if he had just sprouted horns. "I wouldn't call that a lack of concern for material possessions, but rather a lack of respect for them. And that's every bit as bad as overvaluing them."

Bowman's smile faded as he comprehended the extent of her ire. "Miss Appleton, Stony Cross Manor has at least ten different sets of china, each one with enough teacups to help caffeinate all of Hampshire. They're not lacking for cups here."

"That makes no difference. You shouldn't have broken it."

Bowman gave a sardonic snort. "Have you always had such a passion for porcelain, Miss Appleton?"

Without a doubt, he was the most insufferable man she had ever encountered. "I'm sure you'll consider it a failing that I'm not amused by wanton destruction."

"And I'm sure," he returned smoothly, "that you'll use this as an excuse to avoid walking with me."

Hannah contemplated him for a moment. She knew that he was annoyed with her for placing such importance on the loss of a small item of china that would make no difference in the scheme of things. But it had been the boorish gesture of a rich man, deliberately destroying something for no reason.

Bowman was right—Hannah was indeed strongly tempted to cancel the proposed walk. On the other hand, the cool defiance in his eyes actually touched her. He had looked, for just a moment, like a recalcitrant schoolboy who'd been caught in an act of mischief and was now awaiting punishment.

"Not at all," she told him. "I am still willing to walk with you. But I wish you would refrain from smashing anything else along the way."

She had the satisfaction of seeing that she had surprised him. Something softened in his face, and he looked at her with a kindling interest that caused a mysterious quickening inside her.

"No more smashing things," he promised.

"Well, then." She pulled up the hood of her short cloak and headed to the stairs that led to the terraced gardens.

In a few long strides Bowman had caught up with her. "Take my arm," he advised. "The steps might be slippery."

Hannah hesitated before complying, her bare hand slipping over his sleeve and coming to rest lightly on the bed of muscle beneath. In her efforts to keep from waking Natalie earlier, she had forgotten to fetch her gloves.

"Would Lady Natalie have been upset?" Bowman asked.

"About the broken teacup?" Hannah considered that for a moment. "I don't think so. She probably would have laughed, to flatter you."

He sent her a sideways smile. "There's nothing wrong with flattering me, Miss Appleton. It makes me quite happy and manageable."

"I have no desire to manage you, Mr. Bowman. I'm not at all certain you're worth the effort."

His smile vanished and his jaw tautened, as if she had touched an unpleasant nerve. "We'll leave it to Lady Natalie, then."

They crossed an opening in an ancient yew hedge and began along a graveled path. The carefully trimmed bushes and mounded vegetation resembled giant iced cakes. High-pitched calls of nuthatches floated from the nearby woodland. A hen harrier skimmed close to the ground, its wings tensed in a wide V as it searched for prey.

Although it was rather pleasant to hold on to Bowman's strong, steady arm, Hannah reluctantly withdrew her hand.

"Now," Bowman said quietly, "tell me what you assume my opinion of Lady Natalie is."

"I've no doubt you like her. I think you're willing to marry her because she suits your needs. It is obvious that she will smooth your path in society and bear you fair-haired children, and she'll be sufficiently well bred to look the other way when you stray from her."

"Why are you so certain I'll stray?" Bowman asked, sounding curious rather than indignant.

"Everything I've seen of you so far confirms that you are not capable of fidelity."

"I might be, if I found the right woman."

"No you wouldn't," she said with crisp certainty. "Whether or not you're faithful has nothing to do with the woman. It depends entirely upon your own character."

"My God, you're opinionated. You must terrify nearly every man you meet."

"I don't meet many men."

"That explains it, then."

"Explains what?"

"Why you've never been kissed before."

Hannah stopped in her tracks and whirled to face him. "Why do you . . . how did you . . ."

"The more experience a man has," he said, "the more easily he can detect the lack of it in someone else."

They had reached a little clearing. In the center of it stood a mermaid fountain, surrounded by a circle of low stone benches. Hannah climbed onto one of the benches and walked its length slowly, and hopped over the little space to the next bench.

Bowman followed at once, walking beside the benches as she made a circle around them. "So your Mr. Clark has never made an advance to you?"

Hannah shook her head, hoping he would ascribe her rising color to the cold temperature. "He's not my Mr. Clark. As for making an advance . . . I'm not altogether certain. One time he . . ." Realizing what she had been about to confess, she closed her mouth with a snap.

"Oh, no. You can't leave *that* dangling out there. Tell me what you were going to say." Bowman's fingers slipped beneath the fabric belt of her dress and he tugged firmly, forcing her to stop.

"Don't," she said breathlessly, scowling from her superior vantage point on the bench.

Bowman put his hands at her waist and swung her to the ground. He kept her standing before him, his hands lightly gripping her sides. "What did he do? Say something lewd? Try to look down your bodice?"

"Mr. Bowman," she protested with a helpless scowl. "Approximately a month ago, Mr. Clark was studying a book of phrenology, and he asked if he could feel my . . ."

Bowman had gone still, the spice-colored eyes widening ever so slightly. "Your what?"

"My cranium." Seeing his blank expression, Hannah went on to explain. "Phrenology is the science of analyzing the shape of someone's skull and—"

"Yes, I know. Every measurement and indentation is supposed to mean something."

"Yes. So I allowed him to evaluate my head and make

a chart of any shapings that would reveal my character traits."

Bowman seemed vastly entertained. "And what did Clark discover?"

"It seems I have a large brain, an affectionate and constant nature, a tendency to leap to judgment, and a capacity for strong attachment. Unfortunately there is also a slight narrowing at the back of my skull that indicates criminal propensities."

He laughed in delight. "I should have guessed. It's always the innocent-looking ones who are capable of the worst. Here, let me feel it. I want to know how a criminal mind is shaped."

Hannah ducked away quickly as he reached for her. "Don't touch me!"

"You've already let one man fondle your cranium," he said, following as she backed away. "Now it makes no difference if you let someone else do it."

He was playing with her, Hannah realized. Although it was altogether improper, she felt a giggle work up through the layers of caution and anxiety. "Examine your own head," she cried, fleeing to the other side of the fountain. "I'm sure there are any number of criminal lumps on it."

"The results would be skewed," he told her. "I received too many raps on the head during my childhood. My father told my tutors it was good for me."

Though the words were spoken lightly, Hannah stopped and regarded him with a flicker of compassion. "Poor boy."

Bowman came to a stop in front of her again. "Not at all. I deserved it. I've been wicked since birth."

"No child is wicked without a reason."

"Oh, I had a reason. Since I had no hope of ever becoming the paragon my parents expected, I decided to go the other way. I'm sure it was only my mother's intervention that kept my father from tying me to a tree beside the road with a note reading 'Take to orphanage.'"

Hannah smiled slightly. "Is there any offspring your father *is* pleased with?"

"Not especially. But he sets store by my brother-in-law Matthew Swift. Even before he married Daisy, Swift had become like a son to my father. He worked for him in New York. An unusually patient man, our Mr. Swift. Otherwise he couldn't have survived this long."

"Your father has a temper?"

"My father is the kind of man who would lure a dog with a bone, and when the dog is in reach, beat him with it. And then throw a tantrum if the dog doesn't hurry back to him the next time."

He offered Hannah his arm again, and she took it as they headed back toward the manor.

"Did your father arrange the marriage between your sister and Mr. Swift?" she asked.

"Yes. But somehow it seems to have turned into a love match."

"That happens sometimes," she said wisely.

"Only because some people, when faced with the inevitable, convince themselves they like it merely to make the situation palatable."

Hannah made a soft *tsk-tsk* with her tongue. "You're a cynic, Mr. Bowman."

"A realist."

She gave him a curious glance. "Do you think you might ever fall in love with Natalie?"

"I could probably come to care for her," he said casually.

"I mean real love, the kind that makes you feel wildness, joy, and despair all at once. Love that would inspire you to make any kind of sacrifice for someone else's sake."

A sardonic smile curved his lips. "Why would I want to feel that way about my wife? It would ruin a perfectly good marriage."

They walked through the winter garden in silence, while Hannah struggled with the certainty that he was even more dangerous, more wrong for Natalie, than she had originally believed. Natalie would eventually be hurt and disillusioned by a husband she could never trust.

"You are not suitable for Natalie," she heard herself say wretchedly. "The more I learn about you, the more certain I am of that fact. I wish you would leave her alone. I wish you would find some other nobleman's daughter to prey upon."

Bowman stopped with her beside the hedge. "You arrogant little baggage," he said quietly. "The prey was not of my choosing. I'm merely trying to make the best of my circumstances. And if Lady Natalie will have me, it's not your place to object."

"My affection for her gives me the right to say something—"

"Maybe it's not affection. Are you certain you're not speaking out of jealousy?"

"Jealousy? Of Natalie? You're mad to suggest such a thing—"

"Oh, I don't know," he said with ruthless softness. "It's possible you're tired of standing in her shadow. Watching your cousin in all her finery, being admired and sought after while you stay at the side of the room with the dowagers and wallflowers."

Hannah sputtered in outrage, one of her fists clenching and rising as if to strike him.

Bowman caught her wrist easily, running a finger lightly over her whitened knuckles. His soft, mocking laugh scalded her ears. "Here," he said, forcibly crooking her thumb and tucking it across her fingers. "Don't ever try to hit someone with your thumb extended— you'll break it that way."

"Let go," she cried, yanking hard at her imprisoned wrist.

"You wouldn't be so angry if I hadn't struck a nerve," he taunted. "Poor Hannah, always standing in the corner, waiting for your turn. I'll tell you something— you're more than Natalie's equal, blue blood or no. You were meant for something far better than this—"

"Stop it!"

"A wife for convenience and a mistress for pleasure. Isn't that how the peerage does it?"

Hannah stiffened all over, gasping, as Bowman brought her against his large, powerful form. She stopped struggling, recognizing that such efforts were useless against his strength. Her face turned from him, and she jerked as she felt his warm mouth brush the curve of her ear.

"I should make you my mistress," Bowman whispered. "Beautiful Hannah. If you were mine, I'd lay you on silk sheets and wrap you up in ropes of pearls, and feed you honey from a silver spoon. Of course, you wouldn't be able to make all your high-minded judgments if you were a fallen woman . . . but you wouldn't care. Because I would pleasure you, Hannah, every night, all night, until you forgot your own name. Until you were willing to do things that would shock you in the light of day. I would debauch you from your head down to your innocent little toes—"

"Oh, I despise you," she cried, twisting helplessly against him. She had begun to feel real fear, not only from his hard grip and taunting words, but also from the shocks of heat running through her.

After this, she would never be able to face him again. Which was probably what he intended. A pleading sound came from her throat as she felt a delicately inquiring kiss in the hollow beneath her ear.

"You want me," he murmured. In a bewildering shift of mood he turned tender, letting his lips wander slowly along the side of her throat. "Admit it, Hannah—I appeal to your criminal tendencies. And you definitely bring out the worst in me." He drew his mouth over her neck, seeming to savor the swift, unsteady surges of her breathing. "Kiss me," he whispered. "Just once, and I'll let you go."

"You are a despicable lecher, and—"

"I know. I'm ashamed of myself." But he didn't sound at all ashamed. And his hold didn't loosen. "One kiss, Hannah."

She could feel her pulse reverberating everywhere, the blood rhythm settling hard and low in her throat and in all the deepest places of her body. And even in her lips, the delicate surface so sensitive that the touch of her own breath was excruciating.

It was cold everywhere they pressed, and in the space between their mouths where the smoke of their exhalations mingled. Hannah looked up into his shadowed face and thought dizzily, *Don't do it, Hannah, don't,* and then she ended up doing it anyway, rising on her toes to bring her trembling lips to his.

He closed around her, holding her with his arms and mouth, taking a long hungering taste. He pulled her even closer, until one of his feet came between hers, under her skirts, and her breasts surged tight and full against his chest. It was more than one kiss . . . it was a sentence of unbroken kisses, the hot sweet syllables of lips and tongue making her drunk on sensation. One of his hands moved up to her face, caressing with a softness that sent a fine-spun shiver across her shoulders and back. His fingertips explored the line of her jaw, the lobe of her ear, the color-scalded crest of her cheek.

The other hand came up, and her face was caught in the gentle bracket of his fingers, while his lips drifted over her face . . . a soft skim over her eyelids, a stroke over her nose, a last lingering bite of her mouth. She breathed in a gulp of sharp winter air, welcoming the snap of it in her lungs.

When she finally brought herself to look up at him, she expected him to look smug or arrogant. But to her surprise, his face was taut, and there was a brooding disquiet in his eyes.

"Do you want me to apologize?" he asked.

Hannah pulled back from him, rubbing her prickling arms through her sleeves. She was mortified by the intensity of her own urge to huddle against the warm, inviting hardness of him.

"I don't see the purpose in that," she said in a low voice. "It's not as if you would mean it." Turning from him, she walked back to the manor in hurried strides, praying silently that he wouldn't follow her.

And knowing that any woman foolish enough to become involved with him would fare no better than the shattered teacup on the terrace.

SEVEN

As Hannah went into the entrance hall, the warm air caused her cold cheeks to prickle. She kept to the back of the entrance hall, trying to avoid the crowd of newly arrived guests and servants. It was a prosperous, richly dressed group, the ladies glittering with finery and dressed in fur-trimmed cloaks and capes.

Natalie would be awake soon, and she usually began each day with a cup of tea in bed. With so much activity, Hannah was skeptical that they would be able to summon a housemaid. She considered going to the breakfast room to fetch a cup of tea for Natalie and bring it upstairs herself. And perhaps one for Lady Blandford—

"Miss Appleton." A vaguely familiar voice came from the crowd, and a gentleman came forward to greet her.

It was Edward, Lord Travers. Hannah had not expected him to come to Stony Cross Park for the holidays. She smiled warmly at him, the agitated pressure in her chest easing. Travers was a comfortably buttoned-up man, secure in himself and his place in the world, polite in every atom. He was so conservative in manner and appearance that it was almost surprising to see up close that his face was yet unlined and there was no gray in his close-trimmed brown hair. Travers was a strong man, an honorable one, and Hannah had always liked him tremendously.

"My lord, how pleasant it is to see you here."

He smiled. "And to find you all in a glow, as usual. I hope you are in good health? And the Blandfords and Lady Natalie?"

"Yes, we're all quite well. I don't believe Lady Natalie knew of your imminent arrival, or she would have mentioned it to me."

"No," Travers admitted, "I had not planned to come here. My relations in Shropshire were expecting me. But I'm afraid I prevailed on Lord Westcliff for an invitation to Hampshire." He paused, turning sober. "You see, I learned of Lord Blandford's plans concerning his daughter and . . . the American."

"Yes. Mr. Bowman."

"My desire is to see Lady Natalie happy and well situated," Travers said quietly. "I cannot conceive how Blandford could think this arrangement would be best for her."

Since she could not agree without criticizing her uncle, Hannah murmured carefully, "I also have concerns, my lord."

"Surely Lady Natalie has confided in you. What has she said on the matter? Does she like this American?"

"She is disposed to consider the match, to please Lord

Blandford," Hannah admitted. "And also . . . Mr. Bowman is not without appeal." She paused and blinked as
she saw Rafe Bowman at the far side of the entrance
hall, talking with his father. "In fact, Mr. Bowman is
standing over there."

"Is he the short, stout one?" Travers asked hopefully.

"No, my lord. That is Mr. Bowman the elder. His
son, the tall one, is the gentleman to whom Lord Blandford wishes to betroth Lady Natalie."

In one glance, Travers saw everything he needed to
know. Rafe Bowman was unreasonably good-looking,
the power of his lean, striking form no less evident for
his relaxed posture. His sable hair was thick and wind-
ruffled, his complexion infused with healthy color from
the outside air. Those coal-dark eyes glanced around
the room in cool appraisal, while a faint, ruthless smile
curved his lips. He looked so predatory that it made the
memory of his elusive gentleness all the more startling
to Hannah.

For someone like Lord Travers, a rival such as Bowman was his worst nightmare.

"Oh, dear," Hannah heard him murmur softly.

"Yes."

Evie came into the ballroom carrying a heavy two-
handled basket. "Here are the l-last of them," she said,
having just come from the kitchen, where she and two
scullery maids had been filling small paper cones with
nuts and dried fruit, and tying them closed with red
ribbons. "I hope this will be enough, considering it's
such a l-large t—" She stopped and gave Annabelle a
perplexed glance. "Where is Lillian?"

"Here," came Lillian's muffled voice from beneath the tree. "I'm arranging the tree skirt. Not that it matters, since one can hardly see it."

Annabelle smiled, standing on her toes to tie a little cloth doll on the highest branch she could reach. Dressed in winter white, with her honey-colored hair drawn up in curls and her cheeks pink from exertion, she looked like a Christmas angel. "Do you think we should have chosen such a tall tree, dear? I'm afraid it will take from now until Twelfth Night for us to finish decorating it."

"It had to be tall," Lillian replied, crawling out from beneath the tree. With a few pine needles stuck in her sable hair and shreds of cotton batting clinging to her dress, she didn't look at all like a countess. And from the wide grin on her face, one could tell that she didn't give a fig. "The room is so cavernous, it would look silly to have a short one."

Over the next fortnight several events would take place in the ballroom, including a dance, some games and amateur entertainments, and a grand Christmas Eve ball. Lillian was determined that the tree would be as splendid as possible, to add to the festive atmosphere. However, decorating it was turning out to be more difficult than Lillian had anticipated. The servants were so busy with the household work that none of them could be spared for extra duties. And since Westcliff had forbidden Lillian and her friends from climbing on ladders or high stools, the top half of the tree was, so far, completely bare.

To make matters worse, the new fashion in gowns featured a slim-fitting, dropped-shoulder sleeve that prevented a lady from reaching for anything higher than shoulder level. As Lillian emerged from beneath the tree, they all heard the sound of splitting fabric.

"Oh, bloody hell," Lillian exclaimed, twisting to view the gaping hole beneath her right sleeve. "That's the third dress I've torn this week."

"I don't like this new style of sleeve," Annabelle commented ruefully, flexing her own graceful arms in their limited range of motion. "It's quite vexing not to be able to reach upward. And it's uncomfortable to hold Isabella when the cloth pulls over my shoulder so."

"I'll find a n-needle and thread," Evie said, going to hunt in a box of supplies on the floor.

"No, bring the scissors," Lillian said decisively.

Smiling quizzically, Evie complied. "What shall I do with them?"

Lillian raised her arm as much as she was able. "Cut this side to match the other."

Without batting an eye, Evie carefully snipped a gap beneath the sleeve and a few inches along the seam, exposing a white flash of skin.

"Freedom at last!" Lillian raised both arms to the ceiling like some primitive sun worshipper, the fabric gaping at her armpits. "I wonder if I could start a new fashion?"

"Dresses with holes in them?" Annabelle asked. "I doubt it, dear."

"It's so lovely to be able to reach for things." Lillian took the scissors. "Do you want me to fix your dress too, Annabelle?"

"Don't come near me with those," Annabelle said

firmly. She shook her head with a grin, watching as Evie solemnly held up her own arms for Lillian to cut holes beneath her sleeves. This was one of the things she most adored about Evie, who was shy and proper, but often willing to join in some wildly impractical plan or adventure. "Have you both lost your minds?" Annabelle asked, laughing. "Oh, what a bad influence she is on you, Evie."

"She's married to St. Vincent, who is the worst possible influence," Lillian protested. "How much damage could I do after that?" After flexing and swinging her arms, she rubbed her hands together. "Now, back to work. Where's the box of candles? . . . I'll wire more of them on this side."

"Shall we sing to pass the time?" Annabelle suggested, tying a little angel made of cotton batting and a lace handkerchief onto the tip of a branch.

The three of them moved around the tree like industrious bees, singing the "Twelve Days of Christmas." The song and the work progressed quite well until they came to the ninth day.

"I'm sure it's ladies dancing," Annabelle said.

"No, no, it's lords a-leaping," Lillian assured her.

"It's *ladies,* dear. Evie, don't you agree?"

Ever the peacemaker, Evie murmured, "It doesn't m-matter, surely. Let's just choose one and—"

"The lords are supposed to go between the ladies and the maids," Lillian insisted.

They began to argue, while Evie tried to suggest, in vain, that they should abandon that particular song and start on "God Rest Ye Merry Gentlemen" or "The First Noel."

They were so intent on the debate, in fact, that none of them were aware of anyone entering the room until they heard a laughing female voice.

"Lillian, you dunderhead, you always get that wrong. It's *ten* leaping lords."

"Daisy!" Lillian cried, and went in a mad rush to her younger sister. They were uncommonly close, having been constant companions since earliest memory. Whenever anything amusing, frightening, wonderful, or awful happened, Daisy had always been the first one Lillian had wanted to tell.

Daisy loved to read, having fueled her imagination with so many books that, were they laid end to end, would probably extend from one side of England to the other. She was charming, whimsical, fun-loving, but— and here was the odd thing about Daisy—she was also a solidly rational person, coming up with insights that were nearly always correct.

Not three months earlier Daisy had married Matthew Swift, who was undoubtedly Thomas Bowman's favorite person in the world. At first Lillian had been solidly against the match, knowing it had been conceived by their domineering father. She had feared that Daisy would be forced into a loveless marriage with an ambitious young man who would not value her. However, it had eventually become clear that Matthew truly loved Daisy. That had gone a long way toward softening Lillian's feelings about him. They had come to a truce, she and Matthew, in their shared affection for Daisy.

Throwing her arms around Daisy's slim, small form, Lillian hugged her tightly and drew back to view her.

Daisy had never looked so well, her dark brown hair pinned up in intricate braids, her gingerbread-colored eyes glowing with happiness. "Now the holiday can finally begin," Lillian said with satisfaction, and looked up at Matthew Swift, who had come to stand beside them after greeting Annabelle and Evie. "Merry Christmas, Matthew."

"Merry Christmas, my lady," he replied, bending readily to kiss her proffered cheek. He was a tall, well-formed young man, his Irish heritage apparent in his coloring, fair-skinned with black hair and sky-blue eyes. Matthew had the perfect nature for dealing with hot-tempered Bowmans, diplomatic and dependable with a ready sense of humor.

"Is it *really* ten ladies dancing?" Lillian asked him, and Swift grinned.

"My lady, I've never been able to remember any part of that song."

"You know," Annabelle said contemplatively, "I've always understood why the swans are swimming and the geese are a-laying. But why in heaven's name are the lords a-leaping?"

"They're chasing after the ladies," Swift said reasonably.

"Actually I believe the song was referring to Morris dancers, who used to entertain between courses at long medieval feasts," Daisy informed them.

"And it was a leaping sort of dance?" Lillian asked, intrigued.

"Yes, with longswords, after the manner of primitive fertility rites."

"A well-read woman is a dangerous creature," Swift

commented with a grin, leaning down to press his lips against Daisy's dark hair.

Pleased by his obvious affection toward her sister, Lillian said feelingly, "Thank heaven you're here, Matthew. Father's been an absolute tyrant, and you're the only one who can calm him down. He and Rafe are at loggerheads, as usual. And from the way they glare at each other, I'm surprised they don't both burst into flames."

Swift frowned. "I'm going to talk to your father about this ridiculous matchmaking business."

"It does seem to be turning into an annual event," Daisy said. "After putting the two of us together last year, now he wants to force Rafe to marry someone. What does Mother say about it?"

"Very little," Lillian replied. "It's difficult to speak when one is salivating excessively. Mother would love above all else to have an aristocratic daughter-in-law to show off."

"What do we think of Lady Natalie?" Daisy asked.

"She's a very nice girl," Lillian said. "You'll like her, Daisy. But I could cheerfully murder Father for making marriage a condition of Rafe's involvement in Bowman's."

"He shouldn't have to marry anyone," Swift commented, a frown working across his brow. "We need someone to establish the new manufactories—and I don't know of anyone other than your brother who understands the business well enough to accomplish it. The devil knows I can't do it—I've got my hands full with Bristol."

"Yes, well, Father's made marrying Lady Natalie a

nonnegotiable requirement," Lillian said with a scowl. "Mostly because Father lives for the chance to make any of his children do something they don't want to do, the interfering old—"

"If he'll listen to anyone," Daisy interrupted, "it's Matthew."

"I'll go look for him now," Matthew said. "I haven't yet seen him." He smiled at the group of former wallflowers and added only half in jest, "I worry about leaving the four of you together. You're not planning any mad schemes, are you?"

"Of course not!" Daisy gave him a little push toward the ballroom entrance. "I promise we'll be perfectly sedate. Go and find Father, and if he has burst into flames, please put him out quickly."

"Of course." But before he left, Matthew drew his wife aside and whispered, "Why do they have holes in their dresses?"

"I'm sure there's a perfectly reasonable explanation," she whispered back, and pressed a fleeting kiss on his jaw.

Returning to the others, Daisy hugged Evie and Annabelle. "I've brought loads of gifts for everyone," she said. "Bristol is a marvelous place for shopping. But it was rather difficult to find presents for the husbands. They all seem to have everything a man could want."

"Including wonderful wives," Annabelle said, smiling.

"Does Mr. Hunt have a toothpick case?" Daisy asked her. "I bought an engraved silver one for him. But if he already happens to own one, I do have alternate presents."

"I don't think he does," Annabelle said. "I'll ask him when he arrives."

"He didn't come down with you?"

Annabelle's smile turned wistful. "No, and I hate being parted from him. But the demand for locomotive production has become so great, Mr. Hunt is always buried in work. He is interviewing people to help carry the load, but in the meantime . . ." She sighed and shrugged helplessly. "I expect he'll come after the week's end, if he can free himself."

"What of St. Vincent?" Daisy asked Evie. "Is he here yet?"

Evie shook her head, the light sliding over her red hair and striking ruby glints. "His father is ill, and St. Vincent thought it necessary to visit him. Although the duke's doctors said his condition wasn't serious, at his age one never knows. St. Vincent plans to stay with him at least three or four days, and then come directly to Hampshire." Although she tried to sound matter-of-fact, there was a shadow of melancholy in her voice. Of all the former wallflowers and their mates, Evie's connection with St. Vincent had been the least likely, and the most difficult to fathom. They were not publicly demonstrative, but one had the sense that their private life was intimate beyond ordinary measures.

"Oh, who needs husbands?" Annabelle said brightly, sliding an arm around Evie's shoulders. "Clearly we have more than enough to keep us *very* busy until they arrive."

EIGHT

It was Hannah's particular torture to have been cast as chaperone, and therefore be forced to sit beside Natalie during the musical soirée that evening, while Rafe Bowman took Natalie's other side. The entwined harmonies of two sopranos, a baritone, and a tenor were accompanied by piano, flute, and violins. Many of the older children had been allowed to sit in rows at the back of the room. Dressed in their best clothes, the children sat straight and did their best not to fidget, whisper, or wiggle.

Hannah thought wryly that the children were behaving far better than their parents. There was a great deal of gossiping going on among the adults, especially in the lulls between each musical presentation.

She observed that Rafe Bowman was treating Natalie with impeccable courtesy. They seemed charmed by each other. They discussed the differences between New York and London, discovered they had similar

tastes in books and music, and they both passionately
loved riding. Bowman's manner with Natalie was
so engaging that if Hannah had never encountered
him before, she would have said he was the perfect
gentleman.

But she knew better.

And Hannah perceived that she was one of many in
the room who took an interest in the interactions between Bowman and Natalie. There were the Blandfords, of course, and the Bowman parents, and even
Lord Westcliff occasionally glanced at the pair with
subtle speculation, a slight smile on his lips. But the
person who paid the most attention was Lord Travers,
his expression stoic and his blue eyes troubled. It made
Hannah's heart ache a little to realize that here was
a man who cared very much about Natalie, and with
very little encouragement would love her passionately.
And yet all indications pointed to the fact that she
would probably choose Bowman instead.

*Natalie, you're not nearly as wise as you think you
are,* she thought wistfully. *Take the man who would
make sacrifices for you, who would love you for who
you are and not for what he would gain by marrying
you.*

The worst part of Hannah's evening came after the
entertainment had concluded, when the large crowd
was dispersing and various groups were arranging to
meet in one location or another. Natalie pulled Hannah
to the side, her blue eyes gleaming with excitement. "In
a few minutes, I'm going to sneak away with Mr. Bowman," she whispered. "We're going to meet privately
on the lower terrace. So make yourself scarce, and if

anyone asks where I am, give them some excuse and—"

"No," Hannah said softly, her eyes turning round. "If you're seen with him, it will cause a scandal."

Natalie laughed. "What does it matter? I'm probably going to marry him anyway."

Hannah gave a stubborn shake of her head. Her experiences with Bowman had left no doubt in her mind that he would take full advantage of Natalie. And it would be Hannah's fault for allowing it to happen. "You may meet him on the lower terrace, but I'm going with you."

Natalie's grin faded. "*Now* you've decided to be a vigilant chaperone? No. I'm putting my foot down, Hannah. I've always been kind to you, and you know you're in my debt. So go off somewhere and do *not* make a fuss."

"I'm going to protect you from him," Hannah said grimly. "Because if Mr. Bowman compromises you, you will no longer have any choice. You'll have to marry him."

"Well, I'm certainly not going to consider a betrothal without finding out how he kisses." Natalie's eyes narrowed. "Don't cross me, Hannah. Leave us alone."

But Hannah persevered. Eventually she found herself standing unhappily at the side of the lower terrace while Natalie and Rafe Bowman conversed. Bowman seemed unperturbed by Hannah's presence. But Natalie was furious, her voice lightly caustic as she observed aloud that "One can never talk about anything interesting when a chaperone is present," or "*Some* people can never be gotten rid of."

Having never been the focus of such brattiness from Natalie before, Hannah was bewildered and hurt. If Hannah was in Natalie's debt because the girl had always been kind to her, the reverse was also true: Hannah could have made Natalie's life far less pleasant as well.

"Don't you find it irksome, Mr. Bowman," Natalie said pointedly, "when people insist on going where they're not wanted?"

Hannah stiffened. Enough was enough. Although she had been charged with the responsibility of looking after Natalie and chaperoning her, she was not going to allow herself to be subjected to abuse.

Before Bowman could say anything, Hannah spoke coolly. "I will leave you with the privacy you so clearly desire, Natalie. I have no doubt Mr. Bowman will make the most of it. Good night."

She left the lower terrace, flushed with outrage and chagrin. Since she could not join any of the gatherings upstairs without raising questions concerning Natalie's whereabouts, her only options were to go to bed, or find someplace to sit alone. But she was not in the least sleepy, not with the anger simmering in her veins. Perhaps she could find a book to keep her occupied.

She went to the library, peeking discreetly around the doorjamb to see who might be inside. A group of children had gathered in there, most of them sitting on the floor while an elderly bewhiskered man sat in an upholstered chair. He held a small gold-stamped book in his hands, squinting at it through a pair of spectacles.

"Read it, Grandfather," cried one child, while another entreated, "Do go on! You can't leave us there."

The old man heaved a sigh. "When did they start making the words so small? And why is the light in here so poor?"

Hannah smiled sympathetically and entered the room. "May I be of help, sir?"

"Ah, yes." With a grateful glance, he rose from the chair and extended the book to her. It was a work by Mr. Charles Dickens, titled *A Christmas Carol*. Published two years earlier, the story of redemption had been an instant sensation, and had been said to rekindle the cynical public's joy in Christmas and all its traditions. "Would you mind reading for a bit?" the old man asked. "It tires my eyes so. And I should like to sit beside the fire and finish my toddy."

"I would love to, sir." Taking the book, Hannah looked askance at the children. "Shall I?"

They all cried out at once. "Oh, yes!"

"Don't lose the page, miss!"

"The first of the three spirits has come," one of the boys told her.

Settling into the chair, Hannah found the correct page, and began.

"Are you the Spirit, sir, whose coming was foretold to me?" asked Scrooge.

"I am."

The voice was soft and gentle. Singularly low, as if instead of being so close beside him, it were at a distance.

"Who, and what are you?" Scrooge demanded.

"I am the Ghost of Christmas Past."

Glancing around, Hannah bit back a grin as she saw the children's mesmerized faces, and the delighted shivers that ran through them at her rendition of a ghostly voice.

As she continued to read, the magic of Mr. Dickens's words wrought a spell over them all and eased the doubt and anger from Hannah's heart. And she remembered something she had forgotten: Christmas wasn't merely a single day. Christmas was a feeling.

It certainly would have been no hardship to kiss Lady Natalie. But Rafe had refrained from taking any such liberty, mainly because she seemed so determined to entice him into it.

After Hannah had left the lower terrace, Natalie had been defensive and sheepish, telling him that men were fortunate not to require chaperones everywhere they went, because at times it could be maddening. And Rafe had agreed gravely that it must indeed be quite inconvenient, but at the same time Miss Appleton struck him as tolerable company.

"Oh, most of the time Hannah is a dear," Natalie said. "She can be rather bourgeois, but that is only to be expected. She comes from the poor side of the family, and she's one of four unmarried sisters, no brothers at all. And her mother is deceased. I don't mean to sound self-congratulatory, but had I not told Father I wanted Hannah as my companion, she would have suffered *years* of drudgery looking after her sisters. And since she never spends a shilling on herself—she sends her allowance to her father—I give her my castoffs to wear, and I share nearly everything that's mine."

"That is very generous of you."

"No, not at all," she said airily. "I like to see her happy. Perhaps I was a bit harsh on her a few moments ago, but she was being unreasonable."

"I'm afraid I have to disagree," Rafe told her. "Miss Appleton is a good judge of character."

Natalie smiled quizzically. "Are you saying that she was correct in her assessment of you?" She drew closer, her lips soft and inviting. "That you're going to make the most of our privacy?"

"I hate to be predictable," he told her regretfully, amused by her frowning pout. "Therefore . . . no. We should probably take you upstairs before we cause gossip."

"I have no fear of gossip," she said, laying her hand on his arm.

"Then you clearly haven't yet done anything worthy of being gossiped about."

"Perhaps it's only that I haven't been caught," Natalie said demurely, making him laugh.

It was easy to like Lady Natalie, who was clever and pretty. And it would be no hardship to bed her. Marrying her would hardly be a difficult price to pay, to get the business deal he wanted with his father. Oh, she was a bit spoiled and pettish, to be sure, but no more than most young women of her position. Moreover, her beauty and connections and breeding would make her a wife whom other men would envy him for.

As he walked with her toward the main entrance hall, they passed by the open door of the library, where he had conversed recently with his father. A very different scene greeted his gaze now.

Warm light from the hearth pushed flickering shadows to the corners, spreading a quiet glow through the room. Hannah Appleton sat in a large chair, reading aloud, surrounded by a group of avidly listening children.

An elderly man had nodded off by the hearth, his chin resting on the ample berth of his chest. He snuffled now and then as a mischievous boy reached up to tickle his chin with a feather. But the boy soon left off, drawn into the story of Ebenezer Scrooge and his visitation by a Christmas spirit.

Rafe had not yet read the wildly popular book, but he recognized the story after hearing a few lines. *A Christmas Carol* had been so quoted and discussed that its ever-growing fame had become rather off-putting to Rafe. He had dismissed it as a bit of sentimental candy floss, not worthy of wasting his time with.

But as he watched Hannah, her face soft and animated, and heard the lively inflections of her voice, he couldn't help being drawn in.

Accompanied by the Spirit of Christmas Past, Scrooge was viewing himself as he had been as a schoolboy, lonely and isolated during the holidays until his younger sister had come to collect him.

"Yes!" said the child, brimful of glee. "Home, for good and all . . . Father is so much kinder than he used to be, that home's like Heaven! He spoke so gently to me one dear night when I was going to bed, that I was not afraid to ask him once more if you might come home; and he said

*Yes, you should; and sent me in a coach to
bring you . . ."*

Becoming aware of their presence in the doorway,
Hannah glanced up briefly. She flashed a quick smile at
Natalie. But her expression was more guarded as she
looked at Rafe. Returning her attention to the book,
she continued to read.

Rafe was aware of that same warm, curious pull he
felt every time he was near Hannah. She looked ador-
ably rumpled, sitting in the large chair with one slip-
pered foot drawn up beneath her. He wanted to play
with her, kiss her, pull that shiny hair down and comb
his fingers through it.

"Let's leave," Natalie whispered beside him.

Rafe felt a mild sting of annoyance. Natalie wanted
to go somewhere else and continue their earlier conversation, and flirt, and perhaps have a taste of the adult
pleasures that were so new to her, and so damnably familiar to him.

"Let's listen for a moment," he murmured, guiding
her into the room.

Natalie was too clever to show her impatience. "Of
course," she returned, and went to arrange herself grace-
fully in the unoccupied chair by the hearth. Rafe stood
at the mantel, leaned a shoulder against it, and glued
his gaze to Hannah as the story continued.

Scrooge witnessed more from his past, including the
merry Fezziwig ball. A mournful scene followed, in
which he was confronted by a young woman who had
loved him but was now accepting that his desire for
riches had surpassed all else.

"*. . . if you were free to-day, to-morrow, yester-*
day, can even I believe that you would choose
a dowerless girl . . . choosing her, if for a moment
you were false enough to your one guiding
principle to do so, do I not know that your
repentance and regret would surely follow? I
do; and I release you. With a full heart, for the
love of him you once were . . ."

"*Spirit!*" said Scrooge in a broken voice,
"*remove me from this place.*"

Rafe disliked sentiment. He had seen and experienced enough of the world to resist the pull of maud-
lin stories. But as he stood listening to Hannah, he
felt unaccountable heat spreading through him, and it
had nothing to do with the crackling fire in the hearth.
Hannah read the Christmas story with an innocent
conviction and pleasure that was too genuine for him
to resist. He wanted to be alone with her and listen to
her low, charming voice for hours. He wanted to lay his
head in her lap until he could feel the curve of her
thigh against his cheek.

As Rafe stared at her, he felt the quickening of
arousal, the rising warmth of tenderness, and an ache
of yearning. A terrible thought had sprung to his mind,
the wish that *she* were Blandford's daughter instead of
Natalie. Sweet God, he would have married her on the
spot. But that was impossible, not to mention unfair to
Natalie. And thinking it made him feel every bit the
cad that Hannah had accused him of being.

As Hannah finished the second chapter, and laugh-
ingly promised the clamoring children that she would

read more the following night, Rafe made an unselfish wish for someone else for the first time in his life . . . that Hannah would someday find a man who would love her.

After praising the singers and musicians for their fine performance, and leading a group of ladies into the parlor for tea, Lillian returned to the drawing room. Some of the guests were still congregated there, including her husband, who stood in the corner speaking privately with Eleanor, Lady Kittridge.

Trying to ignore the cold needling in her stomach, Lillian went to Daisy, who had just finished talking with some of the children. "Hello, dear," Lillian said, forcing a smile. "Did you enjoy the music?"

"Yes, very much." Staring into her face, Daisy asked bluntly, "What's the matter?"

"Nothing's the matter. Nothing at all. Why do you ask?"

"Whenever you smile like that, you're either worried about something, or you've just stepped in something."

"I haven't stepped in anything."

Daisy regarded her with concern. "What is it, then?"

"Do you see that woman Westcliff is talking to?"

"The beautiful blond one with the smashing figure?"

"Yes," came Lillian's sour reply.

Daisy waited patiently.

"I suspect . . ." Lillian began, and was startled to feel her throat closing and a hot pressure accumulate behind her eyes. Her suspicion was too awful to voice.

Her husband was interested in another woman.

Not that anything would come of it, because West-cliff was a man of absolute honor. It was simply not in him ever to betray his wife, no matter how acute the temptation. Lillian knew that he would always be faithful to her, at least physically. But she wanted his heart, all of it, and to see the signs of his attraction to someone else made Lillian want to die.

Everyone had said from the beginning that the earl of Westcliff and a brash American heiress were the most improbable pairing imaginable. But before long Lillian had discovered that beneath Marcus's outward reserve, there was a man of passion, tenderness, and humor. And for his part, Marcus had seemed to enjoy her irreverence and high-spirited nature. The past two years of marriage had been more wonderful than Lillian could have ever dreamed.

But lately Westcliff had started paying marked attention to Lady Kittridge, a gorgeous young widow who had everything in common with him. She was elegant, aristocratic, intelligent, and to top it all off, she was a remarkable horsewoman who was known for carrying on her late husband's passion for horse breeding. The horses from the Kittridge stables were the most beautiful descendants of the world's finest Arabians, with an amiable sweetness of character and spectacular conformation. Lady Kittridge was the perfect woman for Westcliff.

At first Lillian had not worried about the interactions between Lady Kittridge and her husband. Women were always throwing themselves at Westcliff, who was one of the most powerful men in England. But then a correspondence had begun. And soon afterward he had gone to visit her, ostensibly to advise her on some financial matters. Finally Lillian had begun to experience the pangs of jealousy and insecurity.

"I . . . I've never been able to quite make myself believe that Marcus is truly mine," she admitted humbly to Daisy. "He is the only person, aside from you, who's ever truly loved me. It still seems a miracle that he should have wanted me enough to marry me. But now I think . . . I fear . . . he might be tiring of me."

Daisy's eyes turned huge. "Are you saying you think that he . . . and Lady Kittridge . . ."

Lillian's eyes turned hot and blurry. "They seem to have an affinity," she said.

"Lillian, that is *madness*," Daisy whispered. "Westcliff adores you. You're the mother of his child."

"I'm not saying that I think he's unfaithful," Lillian whispered back. "He's too honorable for that. But I don't want him to *want* to."

"Has the frequency of his . . . well, husbandly attentions . . . lessened?"

Lillian colored a little as she considered the question. "No, not at all."

"Well, that's good. In some of the novels I've read, the unfaithful spouse pays less attention to his wife after he begins an affair."

"What else do the novels say?"

"Well, sometimes a cheating husband may wear a new scent, or start tying his cravat in a different way."

A worried frown gathered on Lillian's forehead. "I never notice his cravat. I'll have to start looking at it more closely."

"And he develops an untoward interest in his wife's schedule."

"Well, that doesn't help—Westcliff has an untoward interest in *everyone's* schedule."

"What about new tricks?"

"What kind of tricks?"

Daisy kept her voice low. "In the bedroom."

"Oh, God. Is that a sign of infidelity?" Lillian gave her a stricken glance. "How do the bloody novelists know these things?"

"Talk to him," Daisy urged softly. "Tell him your fears. I'm sure Westcliff would never do anything to hurt you, dear."

"No, never deliberately," Lillian agreed, her smile turning brittle. She glanced at a nearby window, out at the cool black night. "It's getting colder. I hope we'll have snow for Christmas, don't you?"

NINE

Although Hannah and Natalie had tacitly decided to put their tiff of the previous evening behind them, the relations between them were still cool the next day. Therefore, Hannah was relieved not to be included when Natalie and Lady Blandford went with a group of ladies on a festive carriage ride through the countryside. Other women had elected to stay at Stony Cross Park, conversing over tea and handiwork, while a sizable contingent of gentlemen had left for the day to attend an ale festival in Alton.

Left to her own devices, Hannah explored the manor at her leisure, lingering in the art gallery to view scores of priceless paintings. She also visited the orangery, relishing the air spiced with citrus and bay. It was a wonderfully warm room, with iron grillwork vents admitting heat from stoves on a lower floor. She was on her way to the ballroom when she was approached by a small boy whom she recognized as one of the children she had read to.

The boy appeared apprehensive and uncertain, hurrying through the hallway in an erratic line. He was clutching some kind of wooden toy in his hand.

"Hello. Are you lost?" Hannah asked, squatting to bring herself to face level with him.

"No, miss."

"What is your name?"

"Arthur, miss."

"You don't seem very happy, Arthur. Is there anything the matter?"

He nodded. "I was playing with something I shouldn't, and now it's stuck and I'll get thrashed for it."

"What is it?" she asked sympathetically. "Where were you playing?"

"I'll show you." Eagerly he seized her hand and pulled her along with him.

Hannah went willingly. "Where are we going?"

"The Christmas tree."

"Oh, good. I was just heading there."

Arthur led her to the ballroom, which, fortunately for both their sakes, was empty. The Christmas tree was quite large, glittering with decorations and treats on the bottom half, but still unadorned on the upper half.

"Something has stuck in the tree?" Hannah asked, perplexed.

"Yes, miss, right there." He pointed to a branch well over their heads.

"I don't see any . . . Oh, good Lord, what *is* that?"

Something dark and furry hung from the branch, something that resembled a nest. Or a dead rodent.

"It's Mr. Bowman's hair."

Hannah's eyes widened. "His toupee? But why . . . how . . ."

"Well," Arthur explained reasonably, "I saw him taking a nap on the settee in the library, and his hair was dangling off him, and I thought it might be fun to play with. So I've been shooting it with my toy catapult, but then it went too high, up into the Christmas tree, and I can't reach it. I was going to put it back on Mr. Bowman before he woke, I truly was!" He looked at her hopefully. "Can you get it down?"

By this time Hannah had turned away and covered her face in her hands, and she was laughing too hard to breathe. "I shouldn't laugh," she gasped, "oh, I shouldn't . . ."

But the more she tried to stifle her amusement the worse it got, until she was forced to blot her eyes on her sleeve. When she had calmed herself a bit, she glanced at Arthur, who was frowning at her, and that nearly set her off again. With a potential thrashing in store, he didn't find the situation nearly as amusing as she did. "I'm sorry," she managed to say. "Poor Arthur. Poor Mr. Bowman! Yes, I'll fetch it down, no matter what I have to do."

The hairpiece had to be retrieved, not only for Arthur's sake, but also to save Mr. Bowman from embarrassment.

"I already tried the ladder," Arthur said. "But even when I got to the top, I still couldn't reach it."

Hannah viewed the nearby ladder appraisingly. It

was an extending ladder, an A-frame made of two sets of steps with a third, extendable ladder braced between them. One would slide the middle ladder up or down to adjust the overall elevation. It had already been raised to its full height.

"You're not very big," Arthur said doubtfully. "I don't think you can reach it, either."

Hannah smiled at him. "At least I can give it a try."

Together they repositioned the ladder close to one of the seating niches in the wall. Hannah took off her shoes. Taking care not to step on the hem of her own skirts, she gamely climbed the ladder in her stocking feet, hesitating only briefly before continuing up the extension. Higher and higher, until she had reached the top of the ladder. She reached for the toupee, only to discover with chagrin that it was approximately six inches out of her reach.

"Blast," she muttered. "It's almost within my grasp."

"Don't fall, miss," Arthur called up to her. "Maybe you should come down now."

"I can't give up yet." Hannah looked from the ladder to the overhanging ledge that surmounted the wall niche. It was about a foot higher than the top rung of the ladder. "You know," she said thoughtfully, "if I were standing on that ledge, I think I could reach Mr. Bowman's hairpiece." Carefully she levered herself up and crawled onto the ledge, pulling the mass of her skirts along with her.

"I didn't know ladies as old as you could climb," Arthur commented, looking impressed.

Hannah gave him a rueful grin. Minding her footing, she stood and reached for the drooping locks of the unfortunate toupee. To her disappointment, it was still too high. "Well, Arthur, the bad news is that I still can't reach it. The good news is, you have a *very* effective catapult."

The boy heaved a sigh. "I'm going to get a thrashing."

"Not necessarily. I'll think of some way to retrieve it. In the meantime—"

"Arthur!" Another boy appeared at the ballroom entrance. "Everyone's looking for you," he said breathlessly. "Your tutor says you're late for your lessons, and he's getting crosser and crosser by the second!"

"Oh, thunderbolts," Arthur muttered. "I have to go, miss. Can you get down from there?"

"Yes, I'll be fine," Hannah called down to him. "Go on, Arthur. Don't be late for your lessons."

"Thank you," he cried, and hurried from the room. His companion's voice floated in from the hallway. "Why is she up there . . . ?"

Hannah inched toward the ladder slowly. Before she climbed back onto it, however, the middle extension collapsed, a loud *clack-clack-clack* echoing through the ballroom. Dumbfounded, Hannah stared at the A-frame stepladder, which was now far, *far* below her.

"Arthur?" she called, but there was no response.

It dawned on Hannah that she was in a fix.

How had her peaceful morning come to this, that she was stuck halfway up the side of the ballroom with no way to get down, and the manor mostly empty? In trying to save Mr. Bowman from embarrassment, she had brought no end of it on herself. Because whoever found her was certainly not going to be quiet about it, and the story would be repeated endlessly until she was the laughingstock of the entire holiday gathering.

Hannah heaved a sigh. "Hello?" she called hopefully. "Can anyone hear me?"

No response.

"*Bollocks,*" she said vehemently. It was the absolute worst word she knew.

Since it appeared she might be in for a long wait before someone came to rescue her, she considered lowering herself to sit on the ledge. But it was rather narrow. If she lost her balance, she was undoubtedly going to break something.

Bored and mortified and anxious, she waited, and waited, until she was certain that at least a quarter hour had passed. Every few minutes she called for help, but the manor was deadly silent.

Just as she felt the gnawing of acute self-pity and frustration, someone came to the doorway. She thought it was a servant at first. He was dressed with shocking informality in black trousers and his shirtsleeves rolled up to reveal powerful forearms. But as he entered the room with a relaxed saunter, she recognized the way he moved, and she closed her eyes sickly.

"It *would* be you," she muttered.

She heard her name spoken in a quizzical tone, and opened her eyes to view Rafe Bowman standing below her. There was an odd expression on his face, a mixture of amusement and bafflement and something that looked like concern.

"Hannah, what the devil are you doing up there?"

She was too distressed to reprove him for using her

first name. "I was fetching something," she said shortly. "The ladder collapsed. What are you doing here?"

"I was recruited by the wallflowers to help decorate the tree. Since the footmen are all occupied, they had need of tall people who could climb ladders." A deft pause. "You don't seem to qualify on either account, sweetheart."

"I climbed up perfectly well." Hannah was red everywhere, from her hairline to her toes. "It's merely coming down that poses a problem. And don't call me 'sweetheart,' and . . . what do you mean, wallflowers?"

Bowman had gone to the ladder and had begun to ratchet up the middle extension. "A silly name my sisters and their friends call their little group. What were you fetching?"

"Nothing of importance."

He grinned. "I'm afraid I can't help you down until you tell me."

Hannah longed to tell him to go away, and that she would prefer to wait for *days* before accepting his help. But she was getting tired of standing on the blasted ledge.

Seeing her indecision, Bowman said casually, "The others will be coming in here momentarily. And I should probably mention that I have an excellent view up your skirts."

Drawing in a sharp breath, Hannah tried to gather her dress more closely around her, and her balance wobbled.

Bowman cursed, his amusement vanishing. "Hannah, *stop.* I'm not looking. Be still, damn it. I'm coming up there to get you."

"I can do it by myself. Just set the ladder close to me."

"Like hell. I'm not going to risk you breaking your neck." Having extended the ladder to full length, Bowman ascended it with astonishing swiftness.

"It might collapse again," Hannah said nervously.

"No, it won't. There's an iron locking bracket on either side of the middle ladder. They probably weren't snapped into place before you climbed up. You should always make certain both brackets are locked before using one of these things."

"I don't plan to climb anything ever again," she said with vehement sincerity.

Bowman smiled. He was at the top of the ladder now, one hand extended. "Slowly, now. Take my hand and move carefully. You're going to put your foot on that rung and turn and face the wall. I'll help you."

As Hannah complied, it occurred to her that the logistics of getting down were a bit more difficult than going up had been. She felt a rush of gratitude toward him, especially since he was being far nicer than she would have expected.

His hand was very strong as it closed around hers, and his voice was deep and reassuring. "It's all right. I have you. Now step toward me and put your foot—no, not there, higher—yes. There we are."

Hannah went fully onto the ladder, and he guided her down until his arms closed on either side of her, his body a hard, warm cage. She was facing away from him, staring through the rungs of the ladder, while he was pressed all along her from behind. As he spoke, his breath was warm against her cheek. "You're safe. Rest a moment." He must have felt the shiver that went through her. "Easy. I won't let you fall."

She wanted to tell him that she wasn't at all afraid of heights. It was just the strange sensation of being suspended and yet held, and the delicious scent of him, so clean and male, and the brace of muscles she could feel through the thin linen of his shirt. A curious heat began to unfold inside her, spreading slowly.

"Will the ladder hold both of us?" she managed to ask.

"Yes, it could easily hold a half-dozen people." His voice was quietly comforting, the words a soft caress against her ear. "We'll go down one step at a time."

"I smell peppermint," she said wonderingly, twisting enough to look at him more fully.

A mistake.

His face was level with hers, those eyes so hot and dark, his lashes like black silk. Such a strong-featured face, perhaps the slightest bit too angular, like an artist's line sketch that had not yet been softened and blurred. She couldn't help wondering what lay beneath the tough, invulnerable façade, what he might be like in a tender moment.

"They're making candy ribbons in the kitchen." His breath was a warm, sweet rush of mint against her lips. "I ate a few of the broken pieces."

"You like sweets?" she asked unsteadily.

"Not usually. But I'm fond of peppermint." He stepped to a lower rung, and coaxed her to follow.

"The hairpiece," Hannah protested, even as she descended with him.

"The what?" Rafe followed her gaze, saw his father's

toupee dangling from a branch, and made a choked
sound. Pausing in his descent, he lowered his head
to Hannah's shoulder and fought to suppress a burst of
laughter that threatened to topple them both from the
ladder. "Is that what you were trying to reach? Good
God." He steadied her with one of his hands as she
searched for her footing. "Putting aside the question of
how it got there in the first place, why were you risking
your pretty neck for a wad of dead hair?"

"I wanted to save your father from embarrassment."

"What a sweet little soul you are," he said softly.

Fearing he was mocking her, Hannah stopped and
twisted around. But he was smiling at her, his gaze caressing, and his expression set off a series of hot flutters
in her midriff. "Hannah, the only way to spare my father embarrassment is to keep him from finding that
damned toupee again."

"It's not very flattering," she admitted. "Has anyone
told him?"

"Yes, but he refuses to accept the fact that there are
two things money can't buy. Happiness, and real hair."

"It is real hair," she said. "He just didn't happen to
grow it himself."

Bowman chuckled and guided her down another
rung.

"Why isn't he happy?" Hannah dared to ask.

Bowman considered the question for so long that
they had reached the floor by the time he answered.
"That's the universal question. My father has spent his
entire life pursuing success. And now that he's richer
than Croesus, he's still not satisfied. He owns strings of

horses, stables filled with carriages, entire streets lined with buildings . . . and more female companionship than any one man should have. All of which leads me to believe that no one thing or person will ever be enough for him. And he'll never be happy."

Once they were on the ground, Hannah turned to face him fully, standing in her stocking feet. "Is that your fate as well, Mr. Bowman?" she asked. "Never to be happy?"

He stared down at her, his expression difficult to interpret. "Probably."

"I'm sorry," she said gently.

For the first time since she had met Bowman, he seemed robbed of speech. His gaze was deep and dark and volatile, and she felt her toes curl against the bare floor. She experienced the feeling she sometimes had when she'd been out in the cold and damp, and came inside for a cup of sugared tea . . . when the tea was so hot that it almost hurt to drink it, and yet the combination of sweetness and searing heat was too exquisite to resist.

"My grandfather once told me," she volunteered, "that the secret to happiness is merely to stop trying."

Bowman continued to stare at her, as if he were intent on memorizing something, absorbing something. She felt an exquisite constriction between them, as if the air itself were pushing them together.

"Does that work for you?" he asked huskily. "The not trying?"

"Yes, I think so."

"I don't think I can stop." His tone was reflective. "It's a popular belief among Americans, you know.

The pursuit of happiness. It's in our Declaration, as a matter of fact."

"Then I suppose you have to obey it. Although I think it's a silly law."

A swift grin crossed his face. "It's not a law, it's a right."

"Well, whatever it is, you can't go looking for happiness as if it were a shoe you lost under the bed. You already have it, you see? You just have to let yourself *be*." She paused and frowned. "Why are you shaking your head at me like that?"

"Because talking with you reminds me of those embroidered quotes they're always putting on parlor pillows."

He was mocking her again. If she'd been wearing a pair of sturdy boots, she would probably have kicked him in the shins. After giving him a scowl, she turned to look for her discarded shoes.

Realizing what she wanted, Bowman bent to pick up her slippers. In a lithe movement he knelt on the floor, his thighs spread. "Let me help you."

Hannah extended her foot, and he placed the slipper on her with care. She felt the light brush of his fingers on her ankle, the smooth fire racing from nerve to nerve until it seemed her entire body was alight. Her mouth went dry. She looked down at the broad span of his shoulders, the way the heavy locks of his hair lay, the shape of his head.

He lowered her foot to the floor and reached for the other. It surprised her to feel the softness of his touch. She had not thought a large man could be so gentle. He fitted the shoe onto her foot, discovered that the top edge of the leather upper had folded under in the back, and ran his thumb inside the heel to adjust it.

At that moment, a few people entered the room. The sound of female chatter stopped abruptly.

It was Lady Westcliff, Hannah saw in consternation. How must the scene have appeared to them?

"Pardon us," the countess said cheerfully, giving a look askance at her brother. "Are we interrupting something?"

"No," Bowman replied, rising to his feet. "We were just playing Cinderella. Have you brought the rest of the decorations?"

"Loads of them," came another voice, and Lord Westcliff and Mr. Swift entered the room, carrying large baskets.

Hannah realized she was in the middle of a private gathering . . . there was the other Bowman sister, Mrs. Swift, and Lady St. Vincent, and Annabelle.

"I've enlisted them all to help finish the decorating," Lillian said with a grin. "It's too bad Mr. Hunt hasn't arrived yet . . . he would hardly need a ladder."

"I'm nearly as tall as he is," Bowman protested.

"Yes, but you don't take orders nearly so well."

"That depends on who gives the orders," he countered.

Hannah broke in uncomfortably. "I should go. Excuse me—"

But in her haste to leave, she forgot all about the A-frame ladder directly behind her. And as she turned, her foot caught on it.

In a lightning-fast reflex, Bowman grabbed her before she could fall, and pulled her against his solid chest. She felt the flex of powerful muscle beneath his shirt. "If you wanted me to hold you," he murmured in a teasing undertone, "you should have just asked."

"Rafe Bowman," Daisy Swift admonished playfully, "are you resorting to tripping women to gain their attention?"

"When my more subtle efforts fail, yes." He released Hannah carefully. "You don't have to leave, Miss Appleton. In fact, we could use another pair of hands."

"I shouldn't—"

"Oh, do stay!" Lillian said with enthusiasm, and then Annabelle joined in, and then it would have been churlish for Hannah to refuse.

"Thank you, I will," she said with a sheepish smile. "And unlike Mr. Bowman, I take orders quite well."

"Perfect," Daisy exclaimed, handing Hannah a basket of handkerchief angels. "Because with the exception of the two of us, everyone else here loves to give them."

It was the best afternoon Rafe had spent in a long time. Perhaps ever. Two more ladders were brought in. The men wired candles onto the branches and hung ornaments where directed, while the women passed decorations up to them. Friendly insults flew back and forth, not to mention flurries of laughter as they exchanged reminiscences of past holidays.

Climbing the tallest ladder, Rafe managed to snatch the dangling toupee before anyone else saw it. He glanced at Hannah, who was standing below. Surreptitiously he dropped it to her. She caught it and shoved it deep into a basket.

"What was that thing?" Lillian demanded.

"Bird's nest," Rafe replied insouciantly, and he heard Hannah smother a laugh.

Westcliff poured an excellent red wine and passed glasses around, even pressing one on Hannah when she tried to refuse.

"Perhaps I should water it," she told the earl.

Westcliff looked scandalized. "Dilute a Cossart Gordon '28? A sacrilege!" He grinned at her. "First try it just as it is, Miss Appleton. And tell me if you can't detect flavors of maple, fruit, and bonfire. As the Roman poet Horace once said, 'Wine brings to light the hidden secrets of the soul.'"

Hannah smiled back at him and took a sip of the wine. Its rich, exquisite flavor brought an expression of bliss to her face. "Delicious," she conceded. "But rather strong. And I may have secrets of the soul that should remain hidden."

Rafe murmured to Hannah, "One glass won't overthrow all your virtues, much to my regret. Go ahead and have some."

He smiled as she colored a little. It was a good thing, he thought, that Hannah had no idea how badly he wanted to taste the wine on her lips. And it was also fortunate that Hannah seemed to have no idea of how much he desired her.

What puzzled him was that she wasn't using any of the usual tricks women employed . . . no flirtatious glances, no discreet strokes or caresses, no suggestive comments. She dressed like a nun on holiday, and so far she hadn't once pretended to be impressed by him.

So the devil knew what had inspired all this lust.

And it wasn't the ordinary sort of lust, it was . . . spiced with something. It was a steady, ruthless warmth, like strong sunlight, and it filled every part of him. It almost made him dizzy.

It was rather like an illness, come to think of it.

As the wine was consumed and the decorating continued, the large room echoed with laughter, especially when Lillian and Daisy tried to harmonize a few lines of a popular Christmas carol.

"If that sound were produced by a pair of songbirds," Rafe told his sisters, "I would shoot them at once to put them out of their misery."

"Well, *you* sing like a wounded elephant," Daisy retorted.

"She's lying," Rafe told Hannah, who was stringing tinsel below him.

"You don't sing badly?" she asked.

"I don't sing at all."

"Why not?"

"If one doesn't do something well, it shouldn't be done."

"I don't agree," she protested. "Sometimes the effort should be made even if the results aren't perfect."

Smiling, Rafe descended the ladder for more candles, and stopped to look directly into her ocean-green eyes. "Do you really believe that?"

"Yes."

"I dare you, then."

"You dare me to what?"

"Sing something."

"This moment?" Hannah gave a disconcerted laugh. "By myself?"

Aware that the others were observing the interaction with interest, Rafe nodded. He wondered if she would take the dare and sing in front of a group of people she barely knew. He didn't think so.

Flushing, Hannah protested, "I can't do it while you're looking at me."

Rafe laughed. He took the bundle of wires and candles she handed to him, and obediently went up the ladder. He twisted a wire around a candle and began to fasten it to a branch.

His hands stilled as he heard a sweet, soft voice. Not at all distinguished or operatic. Just a pleasant, lovely feminine voice, perfect for lullabies or Christmas carols or nursery songs.

A voice one could listen to for a lifetime.

> *Here we come a-wassailing*
> *Among the leaves so green,*
> *Here we come a-wand'ring*
> *So fair to be seen.*
> *Love and joy come to you,*
> *And to you your wassail, too,*
> *And God bless you, and send you*
> *A Happy New Year,*
> *And God send you a Happy New Year.*

Rafe listened to her, barely aware of the two or three candles snapping in his grip. This was getting bloody ridiculous, he thought savagely. If she became any more adorable, endearing, or delectable, something was going to get broken.

Most likely his heart.

He kept his face calm even as he struggled with two irreconcilable truths—he couldn't have her, and he couldn't *not* have her. He focused on marshaling his breathing, stacking his thoughts into order, and pushing away the mass of unwanted feeling that kept flooding over him like ocean waves.

Finishing the verse, Hannah looked up at Rafe with a self-satisfied grin, while the others clapped and praised her. "There, I took your dare, Mr. Bowman. Now you owe me a forfeit."

What a smile she had. It set off sparks of warmth all through him. And it took all his self-control to keep from staring at her like a lovestruck goat. "Would you like me to sing something?" he offered politely.

"*Please,* no," Lillian cried, and Daisy added, "I *beg* you, don't ask him that!"

Descending the ladder, Rafe came to stand beside Hannah. "Name your forfeit," he said. "I always pay my debts."

"Make him pose like a Grecian statue," Annabelle suggested.

"Demand that he give you a l-lovely compliment," Evie said.

"Hmmm . . ." Hannah eyed him thoughtfully, and named a popular parlor-game forfeit. "I'll take a possession of yours. Anything you happen to be carrying right now. A handkerchief, or a coin, perhaps."

"His wallet," Daisy suggested with glee.

Rafe reached into his trouser pocket, where a small penknife and a few coins jingled. And one other object, a tiny metal figure not two inches in height. Casually he dropped it into Hannah's palm.

She regarded the offering closely. "A toy soldier?" Most of the paint had worn off, leaving only a few flecks of color to indicate its original hues. The tiny infantryman held a sword tucked at his side. Hannah's gaze lifted to his, her eyes clear and green. Somehow she seemed to understand that there was some secret meaning to the little soldier. Her fingers curved as if to protect it. "Is he for luck?" she asked.

Rafe shook his head slightly, hardly able to breathe as he felt himself suspended between an oddly pleasurable sense of surrender, and an ache of regret. He wanted to take it back. And he wanted to leave it there forever, safe in her possession.

"Rafe," he heard Lillian say with an odd note in her voice. "Do you still carry that? After all these years?"

"It's just an old habit. Means nothing." Stepping away from Hannah, Rafe said curtly, "Enough of this nonsense. Let's finish the blasted tree."

In another quarter hour, the decorations were all up, and the tree was glittering and magnificent.

"Imagine when all the candles are lit," Annabelle exclaimed, standing back to view it. "It will be a glorious sight."

"Yes," Westcliff rejoined dryly. "Not to mention the greatest fire hazard in Hampshire."

"You were absolutely right to choose such a large tree," Annabelle told Lillian.

"Yes, I think—" Lillian paused only briefly as she saw someone come into the room. A very tall and piratical-looking someone who could only be Simon Hunt, Annabelle's husband. Although Hunt had begun his career working in his father's butcher shop, he had eventually become one of the wealthiest men in England, owning locomotive foundries and a large portion of the railway business. He was Lord Westcliff's closest friend, a man's man who appreciated good liquor and fine horses and demanding sports. But it was no secret that what Simon Hunt loved most in the world was Annabelle.

"I think," Lillian continued as Hunt walked quietly up behind Annabelle, "the tree is perfect. And I think *someone* had very good timing in arriving so late that he didn't have to decorate even one bloody branch of it."

"Who?" Annabelle asked, and started a little as Simon Hunt put his hands lightly over her eyes. Smiling, he bent to murmur something private into her ear.

Color swept over the portion of Annabelle's face that was still exposed. Realizing who was behind her, she reached up to pull his hands down to her lips, and she kissed each of his palms in turn. Wordlessly she turned in his arms, laying her head against his chest.

Hunt gathered her close. "I'm still covered in travel dust," he said gruffly. "But I couldn't wait another damned second to see you."

Annabelle nodded, her arms clutching around his neck. The moment was so spontaneously tender and passionate that it cast a vaguely embarrassed silence through the room.

After kissing the top of his wife's head, Hunt looked up with a smile and extended his hand to Westcliff. "It's good to be here at last," he said. "Too much to be done in London—I left with a mountain of things unfinished."

"Your presence has been sorely missed," the earl said, shaking his hand firmly.

Still holding Annabelle with one arm, Hunt greeted the rest of them cordially.

"St. Vincent is still away?" Hunt asked Evie, and she nodded. "Any word on the duke's health?"

"I'm af-fraid not."

Hunt looked sympathetic. "I'm sure St. Vincent will be here soon."

"And you're among friends who love you," Lillian added, putting her arm around Evie's shoulders.

"And there is v-very good wine," Evie said with a smile.

"Will you have a glass, Hunt?" Westcliff asked, indicating the tray on a nearby table.

"Thank you, but no," Hunt said affably, pulling Annabelle's arm through his. "If you'll pardon us, I have a few things to discuss with my wife." And without waiting for an answer, he dragged Annabelle from the ballroom with a haste that left no doubt as to what would happen next.

"Yes, I'm sure they'll be chatting up a storm," Rafe remarked, and winced as Lillian drove her elbow hard into his side.

TEN

Every common room of the manor was busy after supper. Some guests played cards, others gathered around the piano in the music room and sang, but by far the largest group had gathered in the drawing room for a game of charades. Their shouting and laughter echoed far along the hallways.

Hannah watched the charades for a while, enjoying the antics of competing teams that acted out words or phrases, while others shouted out guesses. She noticed that Rafe Bowman and Natalie were sitting together, smiling and exchanging private quips. They were an extraordinarily well-matched pair, one so dark, one so fair, both young and attractive. Glancing at them made Hannah feel positively morose.

She was relieved when the case clock in the corner showed that it was a quarter to eight. Leaving the room unobtrusively, she went into the hallway. It was such a relief to be out of the crowded drawing room, and not to have to smile when she didn't feel like it, that she heaved a tremendous sigh and leaned against the wall with her eyes closed.

"Miss Appleton?"

Hannah's eyes flew open. It was Lillian, Lady Westcliff, who had followed her out of the room.

"It is a bit of a crush in there, isn't it?" the countess asked with friendly sympathy.

Hannah nodded. "I'm not fond of large gatherings."

"Neither am I," Lillian confided. "My greatest pleasure is to relax in a small group with my friends, or better yet, to be alone with my husband and daughter. You're going to the library to read to the children, aren't you?"

"Yes, my lady."

"That's very nice of you. I heard they all enjoyed it tremendously last evening. May I walk with you to the library?"

"Yes, my lady, I would enjoy that."

Lillian surprised her by linking arms with her, as if they were sisters or close friends. They went along the hallway at a slow pace. "Miss Appleton, I . . . oh, hang it, I hate these formalities. May we use first names?"

"I would be honored for you to call me by my given name, my lady. But I can't do the same. It wouldn't be proper."

Lillian gave her a rueful glance. "All right, then. Hannah. I've wanted to talk with you all evening—there is something highly private I want to discuss with you, but it must go no further. And I probably shouldn't say anything, but I must. I won't be able to get any sleep tonight otherwise."

Hannah was dumbfounded. Not to mention rabidly curious. "My lady?"

"That forfeit you asked of my brother today . . ."

Hannah paled a little. "Was that wrong of me? I'm so sorry. I would never have—"

"No. No, it's not that. You did nothing wrong at all. It's what my brother gave to you that I found so . . . well, surprising."

"The toy solider?" Hannah whispered. "Why was that surprising?" She had not thought it all that unusual. Many men carried little tokens with them, such as locks of hair from loved ones, or luck charms or touch pieces such as a coin or medal.

"That soldier came from a set that Rafe had when he was a little boy. Having met my father, you won't be surprised to learn that he was quite strict with his children. At least when he was there, which thank God wasn't often. But Father has always had very unreasonable expectations of my brothers, especially Rafe, because he's the oldest. Father wanted Rafe to succeed at everything, so he was punished severely if he was ever second best. But at the same time, Father didn't want to be overshadowed, so he took every opportunity to shame or degrade Rafe when he *was* the best."

"Oh," Hannah said softly, filled with sympathy for the boy that Rafe had been. "Did your mother do nothing to intervene?"

Lillian made a scoffing sound. "She's always been a silly creature who cares more for parties and social status than anything else. I'm sure she expended far more thought on her gowns and jewels than she did on any of her children. So whatever Father decided, Mother was more than willing to go along with it, as long as he kept paying the bills."

After a moment's pause, the contempt vanished from Lillian's tone, replaced by melancholy. "We rarely ever saw Rafe. Because my father wanted him to be a serious, studious boy, he was never allowed to play with other children. He was always with tutors, studying or being taught sports and riding . . . but he was never allowed one moment of freedom. One of Rafe's few escapes was his set of little soldiers—he would stage battles and skirmishes with them, and while he studied, he would line them up on his desk to keep him company." A faint smile came to her lips. "And Rafe would roam at night. Sometimes I would hear him sneaking along the hallway, and I knew he was going downstairs or outside, just for a chance to breathe freely."

The countess paused as they neared the library. "Let's stop here for a moment—it's not quite eight, and I'm sure the children are still gathering."

Hannah nodded wordlessly.

"One night," Lillian continued, "Daisy was ill, and they kept her in the nursery. I had to sleep in another room in case the fever was catching. I was frightened for my sister, and I woke in the middle of the night crying. Rafe heard me and came to ask what was the matter. I told him how worried I was for Daisy, and also about a terrible nightmare I'd had. So Rafe went to his room, and came back with one of his soldiers. An infantryman. Rafe put it on the table by my bed, and told me, 'This is the bravest and most stalwart of all my men. He'll stand guard over you during the night, and chase off all your worries and bad dreams.'" The countess smiled absently at the memory. "And it worked."

"How lovely," Hannah said softly. "So that's the significance of the soldier?"

"Well, not entirely. You see . . ." Lillian took a deep breath, as if she found it difficult to continue. "The very next day, the tutor told Father that he believed the toy soldiers were distracting Rafe from his studies. So Father got rid of all of them. Gone forever. Rafe never shed a tear—but I saw something terrible in his eyes, as if something had been destroyed in him. I took the infantryman from my nightstand and gave it to him. The only soldier left. And I think—" She swallowed hard, and a shimmer of tears appeared in her dark brown eyes. "I think he's carried it for all these years as if it were some fragment of his heart he wanted to keep safe."

Hannah wasn't aware of her own tears until she felt them slide down both cheeks. She wiped at them hastily, blotting them with her sleeve. Her throat hurt, and she cleared it, and when she spoke, her voice was rusty. "Why did he give it to *me*?"

The countess seemed oddly relieved, or reassured, by the signs of her emotion. "I don't know, Hannah. It's left to you to find out the significance of it. But I can tell you this: it was *not* a casual gesture."

After composing herself, Hannah went into the library in something of a daze. The children were all there, seated on the floor, consuming sugar biscuits and warm milk. A smile tugged at Hannah's lips as she saw more children clustered beneath the library table as if it were a fort.

Seating herself in the large chair, she ceremoniously opened the book, but before she could read a word, a plate of biscuits was put in her lap, and a cup of milk was offered to her, and one of the girls put a paper silver crown on her head. After eating a biscuit and submitting to a minute or two of carryings-on, Hannah quieted the giggling children and began to read:

> *"I am the Ghost of Christmas Present," said the Spirit. "Look upon me."*

As Scrooge went on his travels with the second Spirit, and they visited the Cratchits' humble but happy home, Hannah was aware of Rafe Bowman's lean, dark form entering the room. He went to a shadowy corner and stood there, watching and listening. Hannah paused for a moment and looked back at him. She felt an anguished clutch of her heart, and a surge of ardent need, and a sense of remarkable foolishness as she sat there wearing a paper crown. She had no idea why Bowman would have come without Natalie to listen to the next part of the story. Or why merely being in the same room with him was enough to start her heart clattering like a mechanical loom.

But it had something to do with the realization that he was not the spoiled, heartless rake she had first believed him to be. Not entirely, at any rate.

And if that turned out to be true . . . had she any right to object to his marriage to Natalie?

For the next two days Hannah searched for an opportunity to return the toy soldier to Rafe Bowman, but with the manor so busy and Christmas drawing near, privacy was in short supply. It seemed that Bowman's courtship of Natalie was running smoothly: they danced together, went walking, and he turned the pages of music for Natalie as she played the piano. Hannah tried to be unobtrusive, keeping her distance whenever possible, staying quiet when she was required to chaperone them.

It seemed that Bowman was making a concerted effort to restrain himself around Hannah, not precisely ignoring her, but not paying her any marked attention. His initial interest in her had vanished, which certainly wasn't a surprise. He had Natalie's golden beauty dangling before him, along with the certainty of power and riches if he married her.

"I do like him," Natalie had told her privately, her blue eyes glowing with excitement. "He's very clever and amusing, and he dances divinely, and I don't think I've ever met a man who kisses half so well."

"Mr. Bowman kissed you?" Hannah asked, fighting to keep her tone even.

"Yes." Natalie grinned mischievously. "I practically had to corner him on the outside terrace, and he laughed and kissed me under the stars. There is no doubt he'll ask me to marry him. I wonder when and how he'll do it. I hope at night. I love getting proposals in the moonlight."

Hannah helped Natalie change into a winter dress of pale blue wool, the skirts heavy and flat-pleated, the matching hooded cape trimmed with white fur. The guests were going on a massive afternoon sleigh ride, traveling across the newfallen snow to an estate in Winchester for a dinner and skating party. "If the weather stays clear," Natalie exclaimed, "we'll be riding home under the stars—can you imagine anything more romantic, Hannah? Are you certain you don't want to come?"

"Quite certain. I want to sit by the hearth and read my letter from Mr. Clark." The letter had been delivered that very morning, and Hannah was eager to peruse it in private. Besides, the last thing she wanted was to watch Natalie and Rafe Bowman snuggle together under a blanket on a long cold sleigh ride.

"I wish you would join the sleighing party," Natalie persisted. "Not only would you have fun, but you could do me the favor of keeping company with Lord Travers and diverting him. It seems that every time I'm with Mr. Bowman, Travers tries to barge in. It's dreadfully annoying."

"I thought you liked Lord Travers."

"I do. But he is so reticent, it drives me mad."

"Perhaps if you corner him, as you did Mr. Bowman—"

"I've already tried that. But Travers won't do anything. He said he *respects* me." Scowling, Natalie had gone to join her parents and Mr. Bowman for the sleigh ride.

Once the sleighs had departed, the horses' hooves tamping down the snow and ice, bells jingling on bridles, the manor and grounds were peaceful. Hannah walked slowly through the manor, enjoying the serenity of the empty hallways. The only sounds were the distant muffled conversations of servants. No doubt they, too, were glad that the mass of guests were gone for the rest of the day and evening.

Hannah reached the library, which was empty and inviting, the air lightly pungent with the scents of vellum and leather. The fire in the hearth cast a warm glow through the room.

Seating herself in the chair by the fire, Hannah removed her shoes and drew one foot up beneath her. She took the letter from Samuel Clark from her pocket, broke the seal, and smiled at his familiar penmanship.

It was easy to picture Clark writing this letter, his face still and thoughtful, his fair hair a bit mussed as he leaned over his desk. He asked after her health and that of the Blandfords, and wished her a happy holiday. He proceeded to describe his latest interest in the subject of inherited characteristics as described by the French biologist Lamarck, and how it meshed with Clark's own theories of how repeated sensory information might be stored in the brain tissue itself, thereby contributing to the future adaptation of species. As usual, Hannah only understood about half of it . . . he would have to explain it later in a way that she could comprehend more easily.

"As you see," he wrote, *"I require your good, sensible companionship. If only you were here to listen to my thoughts as I explain them, I could arrange them more precisely. It is only at times like this, in your absence, that I realize nothing is complete when you are gone, my dear Miss Appleton. Everything seems awry.*

It is my fondest hope that when you return, we will sort out our more personal issues. During the course of our work you have come to know my character, and my temperament. Perhaps by now my meager charms have made some sort of impression on you. I have few charms, I know. But you have so many, my dear, that I think yours will atone for my lack. I hope very much that you might do me the honor of becoming my partner, helpmate, and wife . . .

There was more, but Hannah folded the letter and stared blindly into the fire.

The answer would be yes, of course.

This is what you've wanted, she told herself. An honorable offer from a fine, decent man. Life would be interesting and fulfilling. It would better her to be the wife of such a brilliant man, to become acquainted with the people in his educated circles.

Why, then, did she feel so miserable?

"Why are you frowning?"

Hannah started in surprise as she heard a voice from the library threshold. Her eyes widened as she beheld Rafe Bowman standing there with his habitually negligent posture, one leg slightly bent as he leaned against the doorframe. He was in a perturbing state of undress, his vest unbuttoned, his collarless shirt open at the throat, no cravat anywhere in sight. Somehow the disarray only made him more handsome, emphasizing the relaxed masculine vitality that she found so disturbing.

"I . . . I . . . Why are you walking around half dressed?" Hannah managed to ask.

One of his shoulders lifted in a lazy shrug. "No one here."

"*I'm* here."

"Why aren't you at the sleighing party?"

"I wanted a bit of peace and privacy. Why aren't *you* at the sleighing party? Natalie will be disappointed— she was expecting—"

"Yes, I know," Bowman said without a trace of remorse. "But I'm tired of being watched like a bug under a magnifying glass. And more importantly, I had some business matters to discuss with my brother-in-law, who also stayed behind."

"Mr. Swift?"

"Yes. We went over contracts with a British heavy chemical company for sulphuric acid and soda supplies. Then we moved on to the fascinating topic of palm oil production." He came into the room, his hands tucked casually in his pockets. "We agreed that we'll eventually need to cultivate our own source by establishing a coco palm plantation." His brows lifted. "Care to go to the Congo with me?"

She stared directly into his sparkling eyes. "I wouldn't go with you to the end of the carriage lane, Mr. Bowman."

He laughed softly, his gaze sweeping over her as she stood to face him. "You didn't answer my earlier question. Why were you frowning?"

"Oh, it's nothing." Hannah fumbled nervously in the pocket of her skirts. "Mr. Bowman, I've been meaning to return this to you." Pulling out the little toy soldier, she extended her hand. "You must take him back. I think"—she hesitated—"you've been through many a battle together, you and he." She couldn't help glancing at his throat, where the skin looked smooth and golden. A bit lower, there was a shadow of hair where the open neck of his shirt parted. An unfamiliar, hot flourish of sensation went through her stomach. Dragging her gaze upward, she looked into eyes as rich and dark as exotic spices.

"If I take it back," he asked, "do I still owe you a forfeit?"

A smile struggled upward but didn't quite surface. "I'm not sure. I'll have to consider that."

Bowman reached out, but instead of taking the soldier from her, he closed his hand over hers, trapping the cool metal between their palms. His thumb moved in a gentle sweep over the back of her hand. The touch caused her to draw in a quick, severed breath. His fingers moved upward to close around her wrist, drawing her toward him. His head bent as he looked down at the letter still clasped in her fingers. "What is it?" he asked quietly. "What's worrying you? Trouble at home?"

Hannah gave a wild little shake of her head and forced a smile. "Oh, nothing's worrying me. I've received very good news. I'm—I'm happy!"

A sardonic, slanting glance. "So I see."

"Mr. Clark wants to marry me," she blurted out. For some reason, saying the words aloud sent a chill of panic through her.

His eyes narrowed. "Clark proposed by letter? He couldn't have troubled himself to come here and ask you in person?"

Although it was a perfectly reasonable question, Hannah felt defensive. "I find it very romantic. It's a love letter."

"May I see it?"

Her eyes turned round. "What makes you think I would show you something so personal, and—" She made a little sound of distress as he took the letter from her nerveless fingers. But she didn't try to take it back.

Bowman's face was expressionless as he glanced

over the neatly written lines. "This isn't a love letter," he muttered, tossing it contemptuously to the floor. "It's a damned science report."

"How dare you!" Hannah bent to scoop the letter up, but he wouldn't let her. The toy soldier dropped as well, bouncing on the soft carpet as Bowman gripped her by the elbows.

"You're not actually considering it, are you? That cold-blooded, pathetic excuse for a marriage proposal?"

"Of course I am." Her anger exploded without warning, fueled by some deep and treacherous longing. "He's everything you're not, he's honorable and kind and gentlemanly—"

"He doesn't love you. He never will."

That hurt. In fact, the pain doubled and redoubled until Hannah could hardly breathe. She twisted angrily in his hold. "You think that because I'm poor and ordinary, someone like Mr. Clark couldn't love me. But you're wrong. He sees past—"

"Ordinary? Are you mad? You're the most insanely delicious girl I've ever met, and if I were Clark, I'd have done a hell of a lot more than fondle your cranium by now—"

"Don't mock me!"

"I'd have seduced you ten times over." He deliberately stepped on the letter. "Don't lie to me, or yourself. You're not happy. You don't want him. You're settling for this because you don't want to risk being an old maid."

"That's a fine accusation coming from you, you hypocrite!"

"I'm not a hypocrite. I've been honest with everyone, including Natalie. I'm not pretending to be in love. I don't pretend to want her the way I want you."

Hannah froze, staring at him in astonished silence. That he should admit it . . .

She realized she was breathing much too fast, and so was he. Her fingers curled over his sleeves, against his hard-muscled forearms. She wasn't certain if her grip was exerted to keep him close or hold him away.

"Tell me you're in love with him," Bowman said.

Hannah couldn't speak.

More soft insistence. "Then say you desire him. You should feel that much for him, at least."

A tremor ran all through her, spreading to the tips of her fingers and toes. She took the deepest breath possible, and managed a thin reply. "I don't know."

His expression changed, an odd half-smile coming to his lips, his eyes hot and predatory. "You don't know how to tell if you desire a man, sweetheart? I can help you with that."

"*That* kind of help," Hannah said with asperity, "I do not need." She stiffened as he brought her closer, his big hands sliding from her elbows to hook beneath her arms. Her pulse had gone wild, heat thrumming in every part of her.

He bent to kiss her. She made a halfhearted attempt to wriggle away, causing his mouth to catch at her cheek instead of her lips. Bowman didn't appear to mind. He seemed amenable to kissing any part of her he could reach, her cheeks, chin, jaw, the lobe of her ear. Hannah went still, panting as the kisses slid and skimmed over her hot face. She closed her eyes as she felt his lips catch at hers. Another soft, glancing brush, and another, and finally he closed his mouth over hers, deep and secure.

He tasted her with his tongue, searching slowly, and the voluptuous sensation blotted out every thought or flicker of reason. One arm went around her, and his head turned, and he kissed her more urgently. His free hand came up to her jaw, cradling and angling her face. He withdrew just enough to play with her, the fever-glazed caresses of his mouth coaxing her into openness, licking into the vulnerable heat.

The trembling grew worse, insidious pleasure melting through her like boiling sugar. As he tried to soothe her, the tender parts of her body began to throb beneath her clothes, all the laces and seams and stays cinching and clinging with maddening tightness. She struggled a little, chafing against the artificial restrictions. He seemed to understand. His lips left hers, his warm breath fanning the curve of her ear as his fingers went to her bodice. She heard her own moan of relief as she felt him unfastening her collar, and his reassuring whispers that he would take care of her, he would never hurt her, she must relax and trust him, relax . . . all this while his hand moved stealthily along her front, tugging and unfastening.

He kissed her again, a burning velvet caress that caused her knees to give out entirely. But the slow collapse didn't seem to matter, he was holding her securely and lowering her to the carpeted floor. She found herself sprawled half across him while he knelt amid the abundant rumples of her dress. Her garments had fallen in perplexing disarray, buttons undone and skirts riding up. She made a dazed attempt to restore something, cover something, but the way he kissed her made it impossible to think. He gently arranged her beneath him, his arm a hard support beneath her neck. She relaxed helplessly as his wicked mouth took hers over and over, feasting on the taste of her.

"The sweetest skin . . ." he whispered, kissing her throat, easing her bodice open. "Let me see you, Hannah love . . ." He pulled at the top of her chemise, exposing a pale breast that had been pushed full and high by her underbust corset. It was then that Hannah comprehended that she was on the floor with him, and he was uncovering parts of her that no man had ever seen.

"Wait—I shouldn't—you shouldn't—" But her protest was silenced as he bent over the plush curve, his lips closing over a cold stiffening nipple. Her throat hummed with a low whimper as his tongue swept over her in raw-velvet strokes.

"Rafe," she moaned, the first time she had ever said his name, and he let out a shaking breath and cupped both her breasts.

His voice was deep and rough. "I wanted this the first time I met you. I watched you sitting there with that little teacup in your hand, and I couldn't stop wondering what you tasted like here . . . and here . . ." He suckled each breast in turn, his hands coasting over her writhing body.

"Rafe," she gasped. "Please, I can't—"

"No one's here," he whispered against her prickling flesh. "No one will know. Hannah, sweet love . . . let me touch you. Let me show you how it feels to want someone as much as I want you . . ."

And he waited for her answer, breathing against her

quivering skin, a warm hand covering her breast. She couldn't seem to keep entirely still, her knees flexing, her hips rising in answer to a deep, demanding pulse. She was saturated with sweetness and shame and need. She would never have him, she knew that. His life was set on a far different path from hers. He was forbidden. Perhaps that was the reason for this reckless attraction.

Before she quite knew it, she had reached up and guided his head to hers. He responded immediately, taking her mouth in a ravishing, hard-plundering kiss. His hands slipped beneath her clothes, finding tender pale skin, caressing in ways that made her shiver. A muffled cry escaped her as she felt him pulling at the tapes of her drawers. He touched her taut stomach, a fingertip circling her navel. His hand slid over soft curls, cupped her sex, and gently parted her thighs. She felt herself being stroked, petted, lightly spread, his touch careful and clever as if he were drawing a pattern on a frosted window. Except that the surface beneath his fingertips was not icy glass but soft living skin, flushed and burning with desperate sensation.

She had one blurry glimpse of his dark face above hers, his expression intent with lust. He toyed with her, seeming to savor her writhing agitation, his own color high and fevered. She clutched at him, hips arching, lips parted in a wordless plea. One of his fingers pushed inside her, just past the entrance of her body, and she jerked in shock.

His touch withdrew, the wet fingertip making sly, lingering circles around the aching peak of her sex. He pushed her legs apart wider, and kissed the tips of her breasts. His whisper burned against her skin. "If

I wanted to take you now, Hannah, you would let me, wouldn't you? You'd let me enter you, fill you . . . If I asked you to let me come inside you, and ease you . . . what would you say, sweet darling?" He began a light, torturous massage. "Say it," he murmured. "Say it—"

"Yes." She clutched at him blindly, her breath coming in sobs. *"Yes."*

Rafe smiled, his gaze smoldering. "Then here's your forfeit, sweetheart."

He stroked her in a quick, skillful rhythm, covering her mouth with his to absorb her cries. He knew exactly what he was doing, his fingers wicked and sure. It seemed she might die of the annihilating release. She held and stiffened against it even as the pleasure began to rush, and rush, gaining power and force until she was helpless and consumed and shattered.

Slowly he brought her down, kissing and caressing her twitching body. His finger slid inside her once more, this time slipping easily into the wetness. The feel of the intimate muscles grasping him so firmly seemed to cause him pain. She lifted instinctively to take him, and he groaned and withdrew his finger, leaving her swollen flesh to clench on the emptiness.

Rafe's face was hard and sweat-misted as he took his hands from her. He stared down at her with unconcealed hunger, his eyes narrowed, his chest heaving. His hands trembled as he reached for the top hooks of her corset busk, the buttons of her dress, the disheveled undergarments. But as one of his knuckles brushed against her warm skin, he snatched his hands back abruptly and rose to his feet. "Can't," he said hoarsely.

"Can't what?" she whispered.

"Can't help with your clothes." An unsteady breath. "If I touch you again . . . I won't stop until you're naked."

Staring up at him dizzily, Hannah comprehended that the release, and relief, had been rather one-sided. He was dangerously aroused, to the limit of his self-control. She pulled the chemise higher over her naked breasts.

Rafe shook his head, still staring at her. His mouth was a grim slash. "If you want Clark to do the things I just did to you," he said, "then go ahead and marry him."

And he left her there in the library, as if to stay there a moment longer would have resulted in disaster for them both.

ELEVEN

In Evie's opinion, the sleighing party had been enjoyable but too long. She was tired, her ears still ringing from all the noise and caroling. Evie had laughed and frolicked with the group, staying close to Daisy, whose husband had remained at the manor to discuss business matters with Rafe Bowman.

"Oh, I don't mind at all," Daisy had said cheerfully, when Evie had asked if she was disappointed that Swift had not accompanied them. "It's better to let Matthew clear away his business concerns first, and then he'll be free to give me all his attention later."

"Does he w-work very long hours?" Evie had asked with a touch of concern, knowing that the Bowman's enterprise in Bristol was a massive project involving great responsibility.

"There are days when he must," Daisy had replied prosaically. "But there are other times when he stays home and we spend the day together." A grin had crossed her face. "I love being married to him, Evie. Although it's still all so new . . . sometimes it surprises me to wake up and find Matthew beside me." She had leaned closer and whispered, "I have to tell you a secret, Evie: I complained one day that I'd read all the books in the house, and there was nothing new at the bookshop, and Matthew challenged me to try writing one of my own. So I've started one. I have a hundred pages written already."

Evie had laughed in delight. "Daisy," she had whispered back, "are you going to be a f-famous novelist?"

Daisy shrugged. "It doesn't matter to me whether it's published or not. I'm enjoying writing it."

"Is it a respectable story or a naughty one?"

Daisy's brown eyes danced with mischief. "Evie, why would you even ask? Of *course* it's a naughty one."

Now back in the comfort of her room at Stony Cross Manor, Evie bathed in a small portable tub by the hearth, sighing in relief at the feel of the hot water against her stiff, aching limbs. Sleigh rides, she reflected, were one of those activities that always sounded better in theory than they turned out to be in reality. The seats on the sleigh had been hard and lumpy, and her feet had been cold.

She heard a tap at the door, and the sound of someone entering the room. Since she was shielded from view by a standing fabric screen, Evie leaned back and peeked around the screen's wooden frame.

A housemaid was hefting a dripping metal can with rags tied at the handles. "More hot water, milady?" she asked.

"Y-yes, please."

Carefully the maid poured the steaming water at the end near Evie's feet, and Evie sank deeper into the bath. "Oh, thank you."

"Shall I come back with a warming pan to take the chill from the bed, milady?" The long-handled covered pan was filled with live coals and run between the sheets just before bedtime.

Evie nodded.

The maid left, and Evie stayed in the bath until the heat began to dissipate. Reluctantly she stepped from the tub and dried herself. The thought of going to bed alone—again—filled her with melancholy. She was trying not to pine for St. Vincent. But she woke up every morning searching for him, her arm stretched across the empty place beside her.

St. Vincent was the opposite of everything Evie was . . . elegant, dazzlingly articulate, cool and self-possessed . . . and so wicked that it had once been universally agreed he would be an absolutely terrible husband.

No one but Evie knew how tender and devoted he was in private. Of course, his friends such as Westcliff and Mr. Hunt were aware that St. Vincent had reformed his former villainous ways. And he was doing a remarkable job managing the gaming club she had inherited from her father, rebuilding a faltering empire while at the same time making light of the responsibilities he had assumed.

He was still a scoundrel, though, she thought with a private grin.

Standing from the bath, Evie dried herself and donned a velvet robe that buttoned along the front. She heard the door open again. "Back to w-warm the bed?" she asked.

But the voice that answered wasn't the maid's.

"As a matter of fact . . . yes."

Evie stilled at the sound of a deep, silky murmur.

"I passed the maid on the stairs and told her she wouldn't be needed tonight," he continued. " 'If there's one thing I do well,' I told her, 'it's warming my wife's bed.' "

By this time Evie was fumbling to push the screen aside, nearly pushing it over.

St. Vincent reached her in a few graceful strides, folding her in his arms. "Easy, love. No need for haste. Believe me, I'm not going anywhere."

They stood together for a long, wordless moment, breathing, holding tight.

Eventually St. Vincent tilted Evie's head back and stared down at her. He was tawny and golden-haired, his pale blue eyes glittering like gems in the face of a fallen angel. He was a long, lean-framed man, always exquisitely dressed and groomed. But he had not been sleeping well, she saw. There were faint shadows beneath his eyes, and signs of weariness on his face. The touches of human vulnerability, however, only served to make him more handsome, softening what might otherwise have been a gleaming, godlike remoteness.

"Your f-father," she began, staring at him in concern. "Is he . . ."

St. Vincent cast an exasperated glance heavenward. "He'll be fine. The doctors can't find a thing wrong with him, other than indigestion brought on by rich food and wine. When I left, he was leering and pinching the housemaids, and welcoming a score of obsequious relations who want to sponge off him for Christmas." His hands moved lightly over her velvet-covered back. His voice was very soft. "Have you been a good girl in my absence?"

"Yes, of course," she said breathlessly.

St. Vincent gave her a disapproving glance and kissed her with a seductive gentleness that sent her pulse racing. "We'll have to remedy that immediately. I refuse to tolerate proper behavior from my wife."

She touched his face, smiling as he nipped at her exploring fingertips. "I've missed you, Sebastian."

"Have you, love?" He unfastened the buttons of her robe, the light eyes glittering with heat as her skin was revealed. "What part did you miss the most?"

"Your mind," she said, and smiled at his expression.

"I was hoping for a far more depraved answer than that."

"Your mind is depraved," she told him solemnly.

He gave a husky laugh. "True."

She gasped as his experienced hand slipped inside her robe. "What part of m-me did you miss the most?"

"I missed you from head to toe. I missed every freckle. I missed the taste of you . . . the feel of your hair in my hands . . . Evie, my love, you are shamefully overdressed."

And he picked her up and carried her to bed. The velvet robe was stripped away, replaced by firelight and his caressing hands. He kissed the new rich curve of her stomach, fascinated by the changes in her fertile body. And then he kissed her everywhere else, and entered her with teasing skill. Evie jolted a little at the feel of him, so hard and heavy inside her.

Pausing, St. Vincent smiled down at her, his face flushed with desire. "Sweet little wife," he whispered. "What am I to do with you? Such a short time apart . . . and already you've forgotten how to accommodate me." Evie shook her head, straining to take him in, and her husband laughed softly. "Let me help you, love . . ." And he courted her body with careful, wicked thoroughness, until he had entered her fully and brought her, sighing and trembling, into helpless rapture.

Afterward, as Evie reclined on her side and tried to catch her breath, St. Vincent left the bed and returned with a large, rattling leather case. He set it on the nearby table. "I brought the family jewels," he told her.

"I know," she said languidly, and he laughed as he saw what she was staring at.

"No, love. The other family jewels. They're entailed to the future Duchess of Kingston. But I told my father I'm giving them to you now, since he'll obviously live for a damned eternity."

Her eyes widened. "Thank you, Sebastian. But I . . . I don't need jewelry . . ."

"You do. Let me see them on you." He pulled out ropes of priceless pearls, sparkling necklaces and bracelets and earrings wrought of gold and every imaginable jewel. To Evie's squirmy, giggling embarrassment, he sat beside her and began to adorn her, clasping a sapphire bracelet around her ankle, tucking a diamond into her navel.

"Sebastian—" she protested, while he weighted her

naked body with enough gold and rare gemstones to purchase a small country.

"Be still." His mouth searched between strands of pearls, pausing here and there to lick and bite gently at her skin. "I'm decorating for Christmas."

Evie smiled and shivered. "You're not supposed to decorate *me*."

"Don't discourage my holiday spirit, darling. Now let me show you something interesting about these pearls . . ." And before long, her protests had faded into pleasured moans.

TWELVE

Hannah!" Natalie was in bed, drinking her morning tea. A housemaid was stirring the coals and lighting the grate, giggling as if she and Natalie had just shared an irresistibly funny joke.

Having come in from a long walk outside, Hannah entered the room and smiled at her cousin fondly. "Good morning, dear. Finally awake?"

"Yes, I stayed up much too late last night." A group of the younger guests, including Natalie, had spent the evening playing parlor games. Hannah had neither asked nor wanted to know if Rafe . . . for that was how she now thought of Mr. Bowman . . . had been among them.

In the past few days since their astonishing interaction in the parlor, Hannah had avoided Rafe as much as possible, and she had tried not to speak to him directly. She had gone on many solitary walks and had done much soul-searching, unable to comprehend why Rafe had engaged in such an intimate act with her, why she had allowed it, and what her feelings were toward him.

Although Hannah knew little about physical desire, she understood that it resonated more strongly between some people than others. She couldn't perceive whether Rafe felt the same desire toward Natalie. It made her miserable to contemplate it. But she felt certain he had not made *that* kind of advance to Natalie, at least not yet, or Natalie would have told her.

Above all, she understood that ultimately none of this mattered. For a man in Rafe's position, feelings of desire and attachment would make no difference regarding the course he would take. When he married Natalie, he would no longer be the black sheep of the family. In one fell swoop he would please his father, secure his rightful position, and garner a large fortune.

If he chose someone else, he would lose everything.

A woman who cared about him would never ask him to make such a choice.

That afternoon when Hannah had picked herself up from the library floor and painstakingly restored her clothing, she had acknowledged that she was falling in love with him, and the more she knew of him, the deeper the feelings cut. She had retrieved the little toy soldier, and she carried it in her pocket, a small and private weight. It was her token now—she would not offer it to Rafe again. In the future she would be able to close the piece in her hand and remember the dashing American scoundrel and the attraction that had exploded in a passion she would never forget.

I'm a woman with a past now, she thought, amused and wistful.

Regarding Samuel Clark and his proposal . . . Rafe
had been right. She did not love him. It would be unfair
to Clark if she married him and forever compared him
to someone else. Therefore Hannah resolved to write to
Clark soon and turn down his offer of marriage, much
as she was tempted by the safety of it.

Natalie's merry voice recalled her from her thoughts.
"Hannah! Hannah, are you listening? I have something *delicious* to tell you . . . a few minutes ago, Polly
brought the most astonishing little note—" Natalie
waved a scorched and half-crumpled bit of parchment
in front of her. "You'll blush when you read it. You'll
faint."

"What is it?" Hannah asked, slowly approaching the
bedside.

The young dark-haired housemaid, Polly, answered
sheepishly. "Well, miss, it's part of my chores to polish
the grates and clean the hearths in the bachelor's house
behind the manor—"

"That's where Mr. Bowman is staying," Natalie in-
terjected.

"—and after Mr. Bowman left this morning, I went
to the hearth, and while I was sweeping out the ashes, I
saw a bit of paper with writing on it. So I picked it up,
and when I saw it was a love letter, I knew it was for
Lady Natalie."

"Why did you assume that?" Hannah asked, nettled
that Rafe's privacy should have been invaded in such a
way.

"Because he's courting me," Natalie said, rolling her
eyes, "and everyone knows it."

Hannah turned an unsmiling gaze to the housemaid,

whose excitement had dimmed in the face of her disapproval. "You shouldn't snoop through the guests' things, Polly," she said gently.

"But it was in the hearth, half burnt," the maid protested, flushing. "He didn't want it. And I saw the words and thought it might be important."

"Either you thought it was rubbish, or you thought it was important. Which was it?"

"Am I going to get in trouble?" Polly whispered, turning a beseeching gaze to Natalie.

"No, of course not," Natalie said impatiently. "Now Hannah, don't turn all schoolma'amish. You're missing the point entirely, which is that this is a love letter from Mr. Bowman to me. And it's a rather dirty-minded and odd letter—I've never received anything like it before, and it's *very* entertaining and—" She broke off with a gasp of laughter as Hannah snatched it from her.

The letter had been crumpled up and tossed onto the grate. It had burned all around the edges, so the names at the top and bottom had gone up in smoke. But there was enough of the bold black scrawl to reveal that it had indeed been a love letter. And as Hannah read the singed and half-destroyed parchment, she was forced to turn away to hide the trembling of her hand.

—should warn you that this letter will not be eloquent. However, it will be sincere, especially in light of the fact that you will never read it. I have felt these words like a weight in my chest, until I find myself amazed that a heart can go on beating under such a burden.

I love you. I love you desperately, violently,

*tenderly, completely. I want you in ways that I
know you would find shocking. My love, you don't
belong with a man like me. In the past I've done
things you wouldn't approve of, and I've done them
ten times over. I have led a life of immoderate sin.
As it turns out, I'm just as immoderate in love.
Worse, in fact.*

*I want to kiss every soft place of you, make
you blush and faint, pleasure you until you weep,
and dry every tear with my lips. If you only knew
how I crave the taste of you. I want to take you in
my hands and mouth and feast on you. I want to
drink wine and honey from you.*

I want you under me. On your back.

*I'm sorry. You deserve more respect than that.
But I can't stop thinking of it. Your arms and legs
around me. Your mouth, open for my kisses. I
need too much of you. A lifetime of nights spent
between your thighs wouldn't be enough.*

*I want to talk with you forever. I remember
every word you've ever said to me.*

*If only I could visit you as a foreigner goes into
a new country, learn the language of you, wander past all borders into every private and secret
place, I would stay forever. I would become a
citizen of you.*

*You would say it's too soon to feel this way.
You would ask how I could be so certain. But
some things can't be measured by time. Ask me
an hour from now. Ask me a month from now. A
year, ten years, a lifetime. The way I love you
will outlast every calendar, clock, and every*

toll of every bell that will ever be cast. If only you—

And there it stopped.

Aware of the silence in the room, Hannah endeavored to regulate her breathing. "Is there any more?" she asked in a controlled tone.

"I *knew* you would blush," Natalie said triumphantly.

"The rest was ashes, miss," Polly replied, more guarded.

"Did you show it to anyone else?" Hannah asked sharply, concerned for Rafe's sake. These words had not been meant for anyone to read. "Any of the servants?"

"No, miss," the girl said, her lower lip trembling.

"Heavens, Hannah," Natalie exclaimed, "there's no need to be so cross. I thought this would amuse you, not send you into a temper."

"I'm not in a temper." She was devastated, and aroused, and anguished. And most of all, confused. Hannah made her face expressionless as she continued. "But out of respect for Mr. Bowman, I don't think this should be put on display for others' amusement. If he is to be your husband, Natalie, you must protect his privacy."

"I, protect *him*?" Natalie asked roguishly. "After reading that, I rather think I shall need protection *from* him." She shook her head and laughed at Hannah's silence. "What a spoilsport you are. Go and burn what's left of it, if that will put you in a better mood."

Some men, Rafe reflected grimly, wanted nothing more for their sons than to carry on the same life *they* were having.

After a long and vicious argument that morning, it had become clear to him that Thomas would not yield in any way. Rafe must step into the life that his father had planned for him and become, more or less, a reflection of Thomas Bowman. Anything less and his father would regard him as a failure, both as a son and as a man.

The argument had begun when Thomas had told Rafe that he was expected to propose to Lady Natalie by Christmas Eve. "Lord Blandford and I want to announce the betrothal of our children at the Christmas Eve ball."

"What a wonderful idea," Rafe had marveled sarcastically. "But I haven't yet decided whether or not I want to marry her."

The predictable color had begun to rise in Thomas Bowman's face. "It's time to make a decision. You have all the necessary information. You've spent enough time with her to be able to assess her qualities. She's a daughter of the peerage. You know all the rewards that will come your way when you marry. Hell and damnation, why do you even hesitate?"

"I don't have any feelings for her."

"So much the better! It will be a steady marriage. It is time to take your place in the world as a man, Rafe." Thomas had made a visible effort to control his temper as he tried to make himself understood. "Love passes. Beauty fades. Life is not a romantic romp through a meadow."

"My God, that's inspiring."

"You've never done as I asked. You never even tried. I wanted a son who would be a help to me, who would understand the importance of what I was doing."

"I understand that you want to build an empire," Rafe had said quietly. "And I've tried to find a place for myself in your grand scheme. I could do a hell of a lot for the company, and you know it. What I don't understand is why you want me to prove myself this way first."

"I want you to demonstrate your commitment to me. As Matthew Swift did. *He* married the woman I chose for him."

"He happened to be in love with Daisy," Rafe snapped.

"And so could you be, with Lady Natalie. But in the end, love doesn't matter. Men like us marry women who will either further our ambitions, or at least not hinder them. You see what a long and productive marriage your mother and I have had."

"Thirty years," Rafe agreed. "And you and Mother can barely stand to be in the same room together." Sighing tautly, Rafe dragged his hand through his hair. He glanced at his father's round, obstinate face, with its bristling mustache, and he wondered why Thomas had always been compelled to exert such relentless control over the people around him. "What's all this for, Father? What reward do you have after all these years of building a fortune? You take no pleasure in your family. You have the temperament of a baited badger—and that's on your good days. You don't seem to enjoy much of anything."

"I enjoy being Thomas Bowman."

"I'm glad of it. But I don't think I would enjoy it."

Thomas stared at him for a long moment. His face softened, and for once, he spoke in a near-fatherly tone. "I'm trying to help you. I wouldn't ask you to do something I believed to be against your own interests. My judgment about Swift and Daisy was correct, wasn't it?"

"By some miracle of God, yes," Rafe muttered.

"It will all get better, easier, once you start making the right choices. You must build a good life for yourself, Rafe. Take your place at the table. There is nothing wrong with Blandford's daughter. Everyone wants this match. Lady Natalie has made it clear to all and sundry that she is amenable. And you led me to believe that you would go through with it as long as the girl was acceptable!"

"You're right. At first it didn't matter whom I married. But now I find myself unwilling to pick a wife with no more care than I would exert in choosing a pair of shoes."

Thomas had looked exasperated. "What has changed since you arrived in England?"

Rafe didn't answer.

"Is it that brown-haired girl?" his father prodded. "Lady Natalie's companion?"

He looked at his father alertly. "Why do you ask?"

"It seems you've gone more than once to listen to her read at night to a group of children. And you care nothing for children or Christmas stories." The heavy mustache twitched contemptuously. "She's common, Rafe."

"And we're not? Grandmother was a dockside washwoman, and the devil knows who your father was. And that was just on your side of the—"

"I have spent my life trying to elevate this blighted family into something more! Don't use this girl as a way to avoid your responsibilities. You can have as many of her kind as you desire after you've married Lady Natalie. No one would condemn you for it, especially in England. Seduce her. Make her your mistress. I'll even buy a house for her, if that will please you."

"Thank you, but I can afford my own mistresses." Rafe threw his father a glance of dark disgust. "You want this marriage so much that you're willing to finance the corruption of an innocent girl to accomplish it?"

"Everyone loses their innocence sooner or later." As Thomas saw Rafe's expression, his eyes had turned cold. "If you foil everyone's expectations, and embarrass me in the bargain, I will cut you off. No more chances. You will be disinherited, and renounced."

"Understood," Rafe had said curtly.

THIRTEEN

. . . and it was always said of him, that he knew how to keep Christmas well, if any man alive possessed the knowledge. May that be truly said of us, and all of us! And so, as Tiny Tim observed, God Bless Us, Every One!

Glancing upward as she finished reading *A Christmas Carol*, Hannah saw the rapt faces of the children, their eyes shining. There was a brief silence, the shared pleasure of a wonderful story tinged with the regret that it had to end. And then they were all standing, moving about the room, their faces sticky with milk and cookie crumbs, their small hands clapping enthusiastically.

There were two imps on her lap, and one hugging her neck from behind the chair. Hannah looked up as Rafe Bowman approached her. The rhythm of her heart went wild, and she knew her shortness of breath had nothing to do with the small arms clamped around her neck.

His gaze strayed to her disordered clothes and tousled coiffure. "Well done," he murmured. "You've made it feel like Christmas. For everyone."

"Thank you," she whispered, trying not to think of his hands on her skin, his mouth—

"I need to talk to you."

Carefully Hannah dislodged the children from her lap and disentangled the arms from her neck. Standing to face him, she tried in vain to straighten her dress and smooth her skirts. She took a deep breath, but her voice emerged with a dismaying lack of force. "I . . . I don't see how any good could come of that."

His gaze was warm and direct. "Nevertheless, I'm going to talk to you."

The words from his letter drifted through her mind. *"I want to kiss every soft place of you . . ."*

"Please not now," she whispered, with her face flushing and an ache rising in her throat.

Reading the signs of her distress, he relented. "Tomorrow?"

"I need too much of you . . ."

"Yes," she said with difficulty.

Comprehending how deeply his presence unnerved her, Rafe gave her a slight nod, his jaw firming. It seemed there were a dozen things he wanted to say, words hovering impatiently on his lips, but something . . . compassion or pity perhaps . . . afforded him the necessary self-restraint.

"Tomorrow," he repeated quietly, and left her.

* * *

Nannies and nurserymaids came to collect the children, and Hannah went out into the hallway in a daze of misery.

No one had ever told her that love could make every cell in one's body hurt.

She was becoming fairly certain that she would not be able to attend Rafe and Natalie's wedding, that all the events of their married life, the births of children, the celebrations and rituals, would be impossible for her to tolerate. She would stew in jealousy and despair and resentment until she disintegrated. The common wisdom for a woman in her situation was that someday she would meet another man, and she would forget all about Rafe Bowman. But she didn't want another man. There was no one else like him.

I'm doomed, she thought.

With her head lowered, she plowed along the hallway, intending to go to her room, where she could mope and cry in private. Unfortunately, walking with one's head down meant one could not precisely see where one was going. She nearly collided with a woman approaching from the opposite direction, someone who walked with a distinctively long, free stride.

They both stopped abruptly, and the woman reached out to steady Hannah.

"My lady," Hannah gasped, recognizing Lillian. "Oh . . . I'm so sorry . . . I beg your pardon . . ."

"No harm done," the countess assured her. "My fault, actually. I was hurrying to tell the housekeeper something before I had to meet my sister, and—" She paused and stared at Hannah closely. "You look ready to cry," she said bluntly. "Is something the matter?"

"No," Hannah said brightly, and a few hot tears spilled out. She sighed and bent her head again. "Oh, *bollocks*. Forgive me, I must go—"

"You poor thing," Lillian said with genuine sympathy, seeming not at all shocked by the profanity. "Come with me. There's a private parlor upstairs where we can talk."

"I can't," Hannah whispered. "My lady, forgive me, but you're the last person I can confide in about this."

"Oh." The countess's eyes, the same velvet brown as her brother's, widened slightly. "It's Rafe, isn't it?"

More tears, welling up no matter how tightly she closed her eyes against them.

"Is there a friend you can talk to?" Lillian asked softly.

"Natalie is my best friend," Hannah said between sniffles. "So that's impossible."

"Then let me be your friend. I'm not sure I can help—but at least I can try to understand."

They went to a cozy parlor upstairs, a private receiving room decorated in a plush, feminine style. Lillian closed the door, brought Hannah a handkerchief, and sat beside her on the settee. "I insist that you call me Lillian," she said. "And before either of us says a word, let me assure you that everything in this parlor will remain completely private. No one will know."

"Yes, my—Lillian." Hannah blew her nose and sighed.

"Now, what happened to make you cry?"

"It's Mr. Bowman . . . Rafe . . ." She could not seem to put her words in the proper order, and so she let them tumble out, even knowing Lillian would never be able to make sense of them. "He is so . . . and I've never . . . and when he kissed me I thought *no,* it's merely infatuation, but . . . and then Mr. Clark proposed, and I realized I couldn't accept because . . . and I know it's too soon. Too fast. But the worst part is the letter, because I don't even know who he wrote it for!" She went on and on, trying desperately to make herself understood. Somehow, miraculously, Lillian managed to make sense of the mess.

While Hannah poured out the whole story, or at least an expurgated version, Lillian gripped her hands firmly. As Hannah paused to blow her nose again, Lillian said, "I'm going to ring for tea. With brandy."

She pulled the servants' bell, and when a maid came to the door, Lillian cracked it open and murmured to her. The maid went to fetch the tea.

Just as Lillian returned to the settee, the door opened, and Daisy Swift poked her head inside. She looked mildly surprised to see Hannah sitting there with Lillian. "Hello. Lillian, you were supposed to play cards."

"Hang it, I forgot."

Daisy's brown eyes were filled with curiosity and sympathy as she glanced at Hannah. "Why are you crying? Is there something I can do?"

"This is a very private and highly sensitive matter," Lillian told her. "Hannah's confiding in me."

"Oh, confide in me, too!" Daisy said earnestly, coming into the room. "I can keep a secret. Better than Lillian, as a matter of fact."

Without giving Hannah a chance to respond, Daisy closed the door and came to sit beside her sister.

"You are to tell *no one*," Lillian said to Daisy sternly. "Hannah is in love with Rafe, and he's going to propose to Lady Natalie. Except that he's in love with Hannah."

"I'm not sure about that," Hannah said in a muffled voice. "It's just . . . the letter . . ."

"Do you still have it? May I see it?"

Hannah regarded her doubtfully. "It's very private. He didn't want anyone to read it."

"Then he should have burned the damn thing properly," Lillian said.

"Do show us, Hannah," Daisy urged. "It will go no further, I promise."

Carefully Hannah pulled the scrap of parchment from her pocket and gave it to Lillian. The sisters bent over it intently.

"Oh, my," she heard Daisy murmur.

"He doesn't mince words, does he?" Lillian asked dryly, her brows lifting. She glanced at Hannah. "This is Rafe's handwriting, and I've no doubt he was the author. But it is unusual for him to express himself in such a manner."

"I'm sure he knows many pretty phrases to attract women," Hannah mumbled. "He's a rake."

"Well, yes, he's a rake, but to be so open and effusive . . . that's not like him. He's usually—"

"A rake of few words," Daisy finished for her.

"My point is, he was clearly moved by a very strong feeling," Lillian told Hannah. She turned to her younger sister. "What do you think, Daisy?"

"Well, reading such sentiments from one's brother is slightly revolting," Daisy said. "Wine and honey, et cetera. But regardless of that, it's clear that Rafe has fallen in love for the first time in his life."

"The letter may not have been meant for me—" Hannah began, when the door opened again.

It was Evie, Lady St. Vincent, her red hair arranged in a loose chignon. "I've been looking for you," she said.

"We haven't seen you for days," Lillian said. "Where have you been?"

Evie's color deepened. "With St. Vincent."

"What have you been . . . Oh, good God. Never mind."

Evie's gaze fell on Hannah. "Oh, dear. Are you all right?"

"We're discussing something *highly* private," Daisy told her. "Hannah's in love with Rafe. It's a secret. Come in."

Evie entered the room and sat in a nearby chair, while Lillian succinctly explained the situation. "May I see the letter?" she asked.

"I don't think—" Hannah began, but Daisy had already given it to her.

"Don't worry," Lillian murmured to Hannah. "Evie's better than anyone at keeping secrets."

After Evie had finished reading, looking up with round blue eyes, Hannah said morosely, "It may not have been intended for me. It could just as easily have been written for Natalie. Men adore her. They're *always* proposing to her, and she manages them so well, and I can't manage them at all."

"N-no one can manage men," Evie told her firmly. "They c-can't even manage themselves."

"That's right," Lillian said. "And furthermore, any woman who thinks she can manage men shouldn't be allowed to have one."

"Annabelle can manage them," Daisy said reflectively. "Although she would deny it."

There was a brief tap at the door.

"The tea," Lillian said.

However, it was not a maid, but Annabelle Hunt. "Hello," she said with a smile, her gaze sweeping across the group. "What are we doing?" As she looked at Hannah, her expression softened with concern. "Oh, you've been crying."

"She's in love with Rafe Bowman," Evie said. "It's a s-secret. Come in."

"Tell *no one,* Annabelle," Lillian said severely. "This is confidential."

"She's not very good with secrets," Daisy said.

"I am, too," Annabelle said, coming into the parlor. "At least, I am good at keeping big secrets. It's the little ones I seem to have a problem with."

"This is a big one," Lillian told her.

Hannah waited with resignation as the situation was explained to Annabelle.

Receiving the letter, Annabelle scanned the scorched parchment, and a faint smile came to her lips. "Oh, how lovely." She looked up at Hannah. "This was not meant for Lady Natalie," she said decisively. "Hannah, Rafe's attraction to you has not gone unnoticed. In fact, it has been discreetly remarked upon."

"She means everyone's gossiping about you," Daisy said to Hannah.

"I believe," Annabelle continued, "that Rafe likes

Lady Natalie—there is certainly much about her to like. But he loves *you*."

"But it's impossible," Hannah said, her face drawn with miserable tightness.

"Impossible that he could love you?" Daisy asked. "Or impossible because of the infernal deal that Father has set up for him?"

"Both," Hannah said dolefully. "First, I don't know if what he feels for me is merely infatuation . . ." She paused to blot her burning eyes.

" 'Ask me an hour from now,' " Annabelle read softly from the letter. " 'Ask me a month from now. A year, ten years, a lifetime . . .' That's not infatuation, Hannah."

"But even if it's true," Hannah said, "I would never accept him, because he would lose everything, including his relationship with his father. I would not want him to make such a sacrifice."

"Neither should Father," Lillian said darkly.

"Perhaps I should mention," Daisy volunteered, "that Matthew is determined to have it out with Father on this issue. He says Father can't be allowed to run to such excesses. Limits must be set, or he'll try to trample over *everyone*. And since Matthew has a great deal of influence with Father, it's very possible that he can make him retract his demands."

"But no matter what," Annabelle told Hannah, "you have nothing to do with the relationship between Rafe and his father. Your only obligation is to make your feelings known to Rafe. Out of love for him—and for your own sake as well—you must give Rafe a choice. He deserves to know your feelings before he makes important decisions about his future."

Hannah knew that Annabelle was right. But the truth was not exactly liberating. It made her feel hollow and small. She drew the toe of her shoe on a flowered medallion pattern on the carpet. "I hope I can be that brave," she said, more to herself than to the others.

"Love is worth the risk," Daisy said.

"If you don't tell Rafe," Lillian added, "you'll regret it forever. Because you'll never know what might have happened."

"Tell him," Evie said quietly.

Hannah took an unsteady breath, looking at the four of them. They were a peculiar group, all so bright and pretty, but . . . different. And she had the feeling that these women encouraged each other's eccentricities, and relished their differences. Anything could be said or done among them, and no matter what it was, they would accept and forgive. Sometimes, in some rare and wonderful friendships, the bond of sisterly love was much stronger than any blood tie.

It felt nice to be around them. She felt comforted in their presence, especially when she looked into the Bowman sisters' familiar dark eyes.

"All right," she told them, her stomach dropping. "I will tell him. Tomorrow."

"Tomorrow night is the Christmas Eve ball," Annabelle said. "Do you have a nice gown to wear?"

"Yes," Hannah replied. "A white one. It's very simple, but it's my favorite."

"I have a pearl necklace you could borrow," Annabelle offered.

"I have white satin gloves for her," Daisy exclaimed.

Lillian grinned. "Hannah, we'll adorn you more lavishly than the Christmas tree."

The maid brought in tea, and Lillian sent her back for extra cups. "Who wants tea with brandy?" Lillian asked.

"I do," said Daisy.

"I'll take m-mine without the brandy," Evie murmured.

"I'll take mine without the tea," Annabelle said.

Moving to the space beside Hannah, Daisy gave her a fresh handkerchief, and put her arm around her shoulders. "You know, dear," Daisy said, "you're our first honorary wallflower. And we've brought very good luck to each other. I have no doubt it will extend to you, too."

Slightly tipsy from a glass of straight brandy, Lillian said good night to the wallflowers, including their newest member. They all left the Marsden parlor to go to their rooms. Wandering slowly toward the master's suite, Lillian pondered her brother's situation with a troubled frown.

Lillian was a straightforward, blunt-spoken woman, who far preferred to handle a problem by bringing it out into the open and dealing with it directly. But she understood that this matter must be handled with discretion and sensitivity. Which meant she needed to stay out of it. And yet she longed for Rafe to find the happiness he deserved. Even more, she longed to shake her stubborn ass of a father and command him to stop manipulating the lives of everyone around him.

She decided to talk to Westcliff, who could always be

counted on for comfort and common sense. She could hardly wait to hear his opinions on the matter of Rafe and Hannah and Lady Natalie. Guessing that he would still be downstairs with the guests, she headed toward the grand staircase.

As she reached the top of the grand staircase and prepared to descend, she saw her husband standing in the entrance hall below, talking to someone.

Lady Kittridge . . . *again.*

"Marcus," she whispered, feeling a sick pang of jealousy. Followed swiftly by rage.

By God, this was not to be endured. She would not lose her husband's affections to someone else. Not without a fight. Her hands clenched into fists. Although every instinct screamed for her to storm downstairs and jump between her husband and the blond woman, she managed to restrain herself. She was a countess. She would do the dignified thing, and confront Marcus in private.

First she went to the nursery to say good night to little Merritt, who was snuggled in a lace-trimmed crib, with a nurserymaid watching over her. The sight of her precious daughter calmed Lillian somewhat. She smoothed her hand lightly over the baby's dark hair, drinking in the sight of her. *I'm the mother of his child,* she thought vehemently, wishing she could hurl the words like daggers at the glamorous Lady Kittridge. *I'm his wife. And he hasn't fallen out of love with me yet!*

She went to the master bedroom, bathed and changed into a nightgown and velvet dressing robe, and brushed out her long sable hair.

Her heart began to thump madly as Marcus entered the room. He paused at the sight of her, the long locks of hair flowing down her back, and he smiled. Here in private, his autocratic demeanor faded away, and the all-powerful earl became a warm, loving, very mortal man.

He stripped off his coat and dropped it onto a chair. His cravat followed, and then he came to stand beside her.

Lillian closed her eyes as his hands came to her head, fingers sliding gently through her loose hair, and his fingertips massaged her temples. She was acutely aware of him, the coiled power of his body, and the dry, sweet outdoors scent of him, like fresh-cut hay. He fascinated her, this complex man with complex needs. Having been raised with the unstinting criticism of her parents, it was no wonder that she occasionally doubted her ability to be enough for Marcus.

"Are you tired?" he asked in that gravel-wrapped-in-velvet murmur, so distinctive and pleasant.

"Just a little." She sighed as his hands slid to her shoulders, working the tension from them.

"You could just lie back and let me have my way with you," he suggested, his dark eyes glowing.

"Yes, but . . . there is something I must talk with you about first." Damn it, there was a quaver in her voice, despite her attempt to sound calm and dignified.

Marcus's expression changed as he heard the distress in her tone. He pulled her up to face him, and he stared down at her with instant concern. "What is it, my love?"

Lillian took a deep breath. Another. Her fear and anger and worry were so great, it was hard to force the words out. "I . . . I should not stand in the way of your . . . pursuits outside of marriage. I know that. I understand how it is with your kind . . . I mean, you've done it for centuries, and I suppose it was too much for me to expect that you—that I—would be enough. All I ask is that you be discreet. Because it isn't easy to watch you with her—the way you smile, and—" She stopped and covered her face with her hands, mortified to feel tears springing to her eyes. Bloody hell.

"My kind?" Marcus sounded bewildered. "What have I done for centuries? Lillian, what the hell are you talking about?"

Her woeful voice filtered out from behind her hands. "Lady Kittridge."

There was a short, shocked silence.

"Have you gone mad? Lillian, look at me. Lillian—"

"I can't look at you," she muttered.

He gave her a little shake. "Lillian . . . Am I to understand that you think I have a personal interest in her?"

The note of genuine outrage in his question made Lillian feel the tiniest bit better. No guilty husband could have feigned such baffled anger. On the other hand, it was never a good idea to provoke Marcus. He was usually slow to anger, but once it started, mountains trembled, oceans parted, and every creature with an instinct for self-preservation fled for cover.

"I've seen you talking with her," Lillian said, taking her hands down, "and smiling at her, and you've corresponded with her. And—" She gave him a look of miserable indignation. "You've changed the way you tie your cravat!"

"My valet suggested it," he said, looking stunned.

"And that new trick the other night . . . that new thing you did in bed . . ."

"You didn't like it? Damn it, Lillian, all you had to do was tell me—"

"I did like it," she said, turning scarlet. "But it's one of the signs, you see."

"Signs of what?"

"That you've tired of me," she said, her voice cracking. "That you want someone else."

Marcus stared at her and let out a string of curses that shocked Lillian, who had a fairly good command of filthy language herself. Seizing her arm, he pulled her with him out of the bedroom. "Come with me."

"Now? Like this? Marcus, I'm not dressed—"

"I don't give a bloody damn!"

I've finally driven him mad, Lillian thought in alarm, as he tugged and pulled her along with him, down the stairs and through the entrance hall past a few bemused-looking servants. Out into the biting December cold. What was he going to do? Toss her off the bluff? "Marcus?" she asked nervously, hurrying to keep pace with his ground-eating strides.

He didn't answer, only took her across the courtyard to the stables, with their central courtyard and drinking fountain for the horses, into the warm central space with rows of superbly appointed horse stalls. Horses stared at them with mild interest as Marcus pulled Lillian to the end of the first row. There was a stall with a large, cheerful red bow tacked at the top.

The stall contained an astonishingly beautiful Arabian mare about fourteen hands high, with a narrow, eloquent head and neck, large lustrous eyes, and what appeared to be perfect conformation.

Lillian blinked in surprise. "A white Arabian?" she asked faintly, having never seen such a creature before. "She looks like something out of a fairy tale."

"Technically she's registered as a gray," Marcus said. "But the shade is so light, it looks like pale silver. Her name is Misty Moonlight." He gave her a sardonic glance. "She's your Christmas present. You asked if we could work on your riding skills together—remember?"

"Oh." Lillian was suddenly breathless.

"It's taken me six damn months to make the arrangements," Marcus continued curtly. "Lady Kittridge is the best horse breeder in England, and very particular about whom she'll sell one of her Arabians to. And as this horse had been promised to someone else, I had to bribe and threaten the other buyer, and pay a bloody fortune to Lady Kittridge."

"And *that's* why you've been communicating so often with Lady Kittridge?"

"*Yes.*" He scowled at her.

"Oh, Marcus!" Lillian was overcome with relief and happiness.

"And in return for my pains," he growled, "I'm accused of infidelity! I love you more than life. Since I met you, I've never even thought of another woman. And how you think I could have the desire for someone else when we spend every bloody night together is beyond my powers of comprehension!"

Realizing that he had been mortally offended and his outrage was increasing by the second, Lillian offered him a placating smile. "I never thought you would actually betray me that way. I was just afraid that you found her tempting. And I—"

"The only thing I find tempting is the idea of taking you to the tack room and applying a saddle strap to your bottom. Repeatedly. With vigor."

Lillian backed away as her husband approached her menacingly. She was filled with a combination of giddy relief and alarm. "Marcus, everything's settled. I believe you. I'm not at all worried now."

"You should be worried," he said with chilling softness. "Because it's clear that unless there are consequences for this lack of faith in me—"

"Consequences?" she squeaked.

"—this problem may arise again in the future. So I'm about to remove all doubt about what I want, and from whom."

Staring at him with wide eyes, Lillian wondered if he was going to beat her, ravish her, or both. She calculated her chances of escaping. Not good. Marcus, with his powerful but agile build, was superbly fit and accomplished. He was as fast as lightning and could probably outmaneuver a hare. Watching her steadily, he removed his waistcoat and tossed it to the hay-covered floor. Picking up a horse blanket from a folded stack, he spread it over a pile of hay.

"Come here," he said quietly, his expression implacable.

Her eyes went huge. Wild, half-hysterical giggles rose in her throat. She tried to stand her ground. "Marcus, there are some things that shouldn't be done in front of children or horses."

"There are no children here. And my horses don't gossip."

Lillian tried to dart past him. Marcus caught her easily, tossing her onto the blanket-covered hay. And as she yelped and protested, he tore the nightgown from her. His mouth crushed over hers, his hands sliding over her body with insolent demand. A cry snagged in her throat as he bent to her breasts, clamping the tips gently with his teeth, then soothing the little aches with his tongue. He did all the things that he knew would arouse her, his lovemaking gentle but ruthless, until she gasped out a few words of surrender. Unfastening his trousers with a few deft tugs, he thrust deeply inside her with primitive force.

Lillian shivered in ecstasy and gripped his muscular flexing back. He kissed her, his mouth rough and greedy, his body moving in a powerful rhythm. "Marcus," Lillian gasped, "I'll never doubt you again . . . oh, God . . ."

He smiled privately against her hair and pulled her hips up higher against his. "See that you don't," he murmured. And long into the night, he had his way with her.

FOURTEEN

Hannah tried in vain to find an opportunity to talk to Rafe the next day. He was impossible to find. And so were Natalie and the Blandfords, and the Bowmans. She had the uneasy feeling that something was brewing.

Stony Cross Manor was swarming with activity, guests singing, eating, drinking, while the children put on productions with a huge toy theater set up in one of the common rooms.

Quite late in the day, Hannah finally caught a glimpse of Rafe as she passed by Lord Westcliff's private study. The door had been left open, and he could be seen inside talking with Westcliff and Mr. Swift. As she paused uncertainly, Rafe glanced in her direction. Instantly he pushed away from the desk he had been leaning against, and murmured to the others, "One moment."

He came out to the hallway, his expression uncharacteristically sober. But a smile tipped the corners of his mouth as he looked down at her. "Hannah." The softness of his voice sent a ripple of awareness down her back.

"You . . . you said you wanted to, talk with me," she managed to say.

"Yes, I did. I do. Forgive me—I've been occupied by a few matters." He reached out to touch her as if he couldn't help it, lightly fingering the loose fabric of one of her sleeves. "We'll need time and privacy for what I want to discuss—both of which seem to be in short supply today."

"Perhaps later tonight?" she suggested hesitantly.

"Yes. I'll find you." Letting go of her sleeve, he gave her a slight, gentlemanly bow. "Until tonight."

When Hannah went upstairs to help Natalie change into her ballgown, and then ready herself, she was mystified to discover that Natalie was already fully dressed.

Her cousin looked magnificent in a pale blue satin gown trimmed with bunches of matching blue tulle, her hair dressed in upswept golden curls. "Hannah!" Natalie exclaimed, leaving their room in the company of Lady Blandford. "I have something to tell you—something very important—"

"You may tell her later," Lady Blandford interrupted, seeming as distracted as her daughter. "Lord Blandford and Lord Westcliff are downstairs, Natalie. It will not do to keep them waiting."

"Yes, of course." Natalie's blue eyes sparkled with excitement. "We'll speak soon, Hannah."

Bemused, Hannah watched them hurry along the hallway. Something was definitely afoot, she thought, and a rush of worry caused a cool sweat to collect beneath the layers of her clothes.

A lady's maid waited for her inside the bedroom. "Miss Appleton. Lady Westcliff sent me to help you get ready for the ball."

"Did she? That is very kind. I don't usually require much help, but—"

"I'm very good at arranging hair," the maid said firmly. "And Lady Westcliff told me to use her very own pearl hairpins for you. Now, if you'll sit at the dressing table, miss . . . ?"

Touched by Lillian's generosity in sending her own maid, Hannah complied. It took an eternity to curl her hair with hot tongs, and arrange it in pinned-up curls, with gleaming white pearls scattered amid the dark locks of her hair. The maid helped her into the white ballgown, and gave her a pair of silver-embroidered silk stockings from Evie. After fastening a pearl necklace from Annabelle Hunt around Hannah's neck, the maid helped her to tug on a pair of long white satin gloves from Daisy Swift. The wallflowers, Hannah thought with a grateful smile, were her own group of fairy godmothers.

They finished with a dusting of powder on her nose and forehead, and some rose petal salve for her lips.

Hannah was vaguely startled by her own elegant reflection, her eyes wide and green, the elaborate coiffure contrasting pleasingly with the simplicity of the white gown.

"Very beautiful, miss," the maid pronounced.

"You'd best hurry downstairs . . . the ball will be start-ing soon."

Hannah was too nervous to be tempted by the magnifi-cent buffet of delicacies laid out on long tables. The refreshments would be enjoyed by the guests during the dance, and later in the evening a formal supper would be served. As soon as she appeared in the ballroom, she was joined by Lillian and Daisy, who exclaimed over her appearance.

"You are both so very kind," Hannah told them ear-nestly. "And to loan me the pearls and the gloves, it is beyond generous—"

"We have ulterior motives," Daisy replied.

Hannah gave her a perplexed glance.

"Very good ulterior motives," Lillian said with a grin. "We want you as our sister."

"Have you spoken to Rafe yet?" Daisy asked sotto voce.

Hannah shook her head. "I've hardly seen him all day. It seemed he was missing for a while, and then he was talking with a great many people."

"Something is brewing," Lillian said. "Westcliff was busy all day as well. And my parents were no-where to be seen."

"The Blandfords as well," Hannah commented ap-prehensively. "What does all that mean?"

"I don't know." Lillian gave her a reassuring smile. "But I'm certain everything will be fine." She slipped her arm through Hannah's. "Come look at the tree."

With all the candles lit, the Christmas tree was a brilliant, spectacular sight, hundreds of tiny flames glowing amid the branches like fairy lights. The entire ballroom was decorated with greenery and gilt and red velvet swags. Hannah had never attended such a dazzling event. She looked around the room in wonder, watching couples swirling across the floor while the orchestra played Christmas music in waltz-time. Chandeliers shed sparkling light on the scene. Through the nearby row of windows, she saw the glow of torches that had been set in the gardens, glowing against a sky the color of black plums.

And then she saw Rafe across the room. Like the other men present, he was dressed in the traditional evening scheme of black and white. The sight of him, so charismatic and handsome, made her light-headed with yearning.

Their gazes caught across the distance, and he surveyed her intently, missing no detail of her appearance. His mouth curved with a slow, easy smile, and her knees turned to jelly.

"Here, miss." A servant had come with a tray of champagne. Glasses of the sparkling vintage were being passed out among all the guests. The orchestra finished a set and paused, and there was a clink of what sounded like silver on crystal.

"What's this?" Lillian asked, her brows lifting as she and Daisy took some champagne.

"Apparently someone is going to make a toast," Daisy commented.

Seeing Lord Blandford draw Natalie with him on the other side of the room, Hannah gripped the stem of her champagne glass tightly. Every nerve tensed with foreboding.

No . . . it couldn't be.

"My friends," Blandford said a few times, attracting the attention of the crowd. Guests quieted and looked at him expectantly. "As many of you know, Lady Blandford and I were blessed with only one child, our beloved Natalie. And now the time has come to give her into the keeping of a man who will be entrusted with her happiness and safekeeping, as they embark upon their life's journey together—"

"Oh, no," Hannah heard Lillian whisper.

The coldness concentrated in her chest until she felt it needling through her heart. Lord Blandford continued to speak, but she couldn't make out the words through the blood rushing in her ears. Her throat closed on an anguished cry.

She was too late. She had waited too long.

Her hands had begun to shake too badly for her to hold the champagne. She thrust the glass blindly at Daisy. "Please take this," she choked. "I can't . . . I have to . . ." She turned in panic and anguish, and made her way to the nearest exit, one of the French doors that led outside.

"On this most joyous of holidays," Blandford continued, "I have the honor and pleasure of announcing a betrothal. Let us now make a toast to my daughter and the man to whom she will bestow her hand in marriage . . ."

Hannah slipped out the door and closed it, desperately pulling in huge lungfuls of cold winter air. There was the sound of a muffled cheer from inside.

The toast was done.

Rafe and Natalie were engaged.

She nearly staggered under the weight of her own grief. Wild thoughts coursed through her mind. She couldn't face it, any of it. She would have to leave to-night and go somewhere . . . back to her father and sisters . . . she could never see Natalie or Rafe or the Blandfords again. She hated Rafe for making her love him. She hated herself. She wanted to die.

Hannah, don't be an idiot, she thought desperately. *You're not the first woman with a broken heart, nor will you be the last. You will survive this.*

But the more she fought for self-control, the more it seemed to elude her. She had to find a place where she could fall apart. She headed out into the garden, fol-lowing one of the torchlit paths. Reaching the little clearing with the mermaid fountain, she sat on one of the hard, freezing stone benches. As she covered her face with her hands, hot tears soaked into the white satin gloves. Each sob tore through her chest with knife-like sharpness.

And then through the wrenching gasps of misery, she heard someone say her name.

For anyone to see her like this was the ultimate hu-miliation. Hannah shook her head and curled into a ball of misery, managing to choke out helplessly, "Please leave me—"

But a man sat beside her, and she was gathered up in warm, strong arms. Her head was pulled against a hard chest. "Hannah, love . . . *no.* No, don't cry." It was Rafe's deep voice, his familiar scent. She tried to push him away, but Rafe gripped her firmly, his dark head bent over hers. Murmuring endearments, he smoothed her hair and pressed kisses against her forehead. His lips brushed her wet lashes. "Come. There's no need for this, sweet darling. Hush, everything is fine. Look at me, Hannah."

The exquisite pleasure of being held by him, comforted by him, made her feel even worse. "You should be back there," she said, and let out a few coughing sobs. "With Natalie."

His palm stroked her back in firm circles. "Hannah. Sweetheart. Please calm yourself enough that we can talk."

"I don't want to talk—"

"I do. And you're going to listen to me. Take a deep breath. Good girl. One more." Rafe let go of her long enough to remove his evening coat, and he wrapped it around her shivering body. "I didn't think Blandford would have made the announcement so damned quickly," he said, pulling her close again, "or I would have made an effort to reach you first."

"It doesn't matter," she said, her despair congealing into sullenness. "Nothing matters. Don't even try to—"

Rafe put his hand over her mouth and looked down at her. Lit by the torches, his face was cast half in shadow, his eyes dark and bright. His voice was thick and warm, and tenderly chiding. "Had you stayed in the ballroom about thirty seconds longer, my impulsive love, you would have heard Blandford announcing Natalie's engagement to Lord Travers."

Hannah's entire body stiffened. She couldn't even breathe.

"With the exception of a brief errand in the village," Rafe continued, "I've been talking with people all damn day. With my parents, the Blandfords, Westcliff . . . and most importantly, Natalie." He took his hand from her mouth and rummaged in the pocket of his coat. Extracting a handkerchief, he wiped her wet cheeks gently. "I told her," he continued, "that as lovely and appealing as I found her, I could not marry her. Because I would never be able to care for her in the way that she deserved. Because I had fallen in love, deeply and forever, with someone else." He smiled into Hannah's dazed eyes. "I believe she went straight to Travers afterward, and in giving her comfort and counsel, he probably confessed his own feelings for her. I hope she hasn't rushed into an impulsive betrothal merely to save face. But that's not my concern."

Cradling Hannah's face in his hands, Rafe waited for her to say something. She merely shook her head, too overwhelmed to make a sound.

"That day in the library," he told her, "when I nearly made love to you, I realized afterward that I had wanted to get caught with you. I wanted to compromise you— anything that would allow me to be with you. And I knew then that no matter what, I wasn't going to be able to marry Natalie. Because a lifetime is too long to spend with the wrong woman."

His head and shoulders blotted out the torchlight as he bent over her, his mouth taking hers with a slow, penetrating kiss. He coaxed her trembling lips to part, exploring her with an ardent tenderness that caused her heart to thump with painful force. She gasped as she felt his hand slide inside the coat, caressing the fine skin exposed by the low-cut bodice of her ballgown.

"Darling Hannah," he whispered. "When I saw you crying just now, I thought 'Please, God, let it be because she cares for me, wicked scoundrel that I am. Let her love me even a little.' "

"I was crying," she managed to tell him unsteadily, "because my heart was breaking at the thought of you marrying someone else." She had to set her jaw against a quiver of emotion. "Because I . . . I wanted you for myself."

The flare of passion in his eyes sent her pulse rioting. "Then I have something to ask you, my love. But first you must understand . . . I'm not going to inherit Bowman's. That doesn't mean I can't provide for you, however. I'm a wealthy man in my own right. And I'm going to take my ill-gotten gains and put them to good use. There are opportunities everywhere."

Finding it difficult to think clearly, Hannah had to concentrate as if she were translating a foreign language. "You've been cut off?" she finally whispered in concern.

Pulling back a little, Rafe nodded. His face was sober and purposeful. "It's for the best. Sometime in the future, my father and I may find a way to accept each other. But in the meantime, I won't live according to any man's dictates."

Her hand stole up to the side of his face, caressing his cheek gently. "I didn't want you to make such a sacrifice for me."

His lashes half lowered at her touch. "It wasn't a sacrifice. It was salvation. My father sees it as a weakness, of course. But I told him it doesn't make me less of a man to love someone this way. It makes me more of one. And you're under no obligation, you know. I don't want you to—"

"Rafe," she said unsteadily, "obligation is no part of what I feel for you."

His expression caused her insides to turn molten. Picking up one of her hands, he removed her glove in a leisurely manner, pulling gently at the fingertips to loosen them. After peeling off the white satin, he kissed the backs of her fingers and laid her palm against his warm, smooth-shaven cheek. "Hannah, I love you almost more than I can bear. Whether you want me or not, I'm yours. And I'm not at all certain what will happen to me if I have to spend the rest of my life without you. Please marry me so I can stop trying to be happy and finally just *be*. I know this has happened very fast, but—"

"Some things can't be measured by time," Hannah said with a tremulous smile.

Rafe went still and gave her a questioning glance.

"One of the housemaids found a half-burned love letter in the hearth in your room," Hannah explained, "and she brought it to Natalie, who showed it to me. Natalie assumed it was for her."

Even in the darkness, she saw Rafe's color heighten. "Well, hell," he said in a rueful tone. Bringing her close, he held her and whispered against her ear. "It was for you. Every word was about you. You must have known when you read it."

"I wanted it to be about me," Hannah said shyly. "And"—her own face flamed—"those things you wrote—I want all of that, too."

He gave a soft laugh and drew back to look at her. "Then give me your answer." He crushed a brief, impassioned kiss against her lips. "Say it, or I'll have to keep kissing you until you surrender."

"Yes," she said, breathless with joy. "Yes, I'll marry you. Because I love you, too, Rafe, I love—"

He seized her mouth with his and kissed her hungrily, his hands coming up to her coiffure and disheveling it. She didn't care in the least. His mouth was so hot, delicious, consuming her with light sensual caresses, then ravaging deep and hard. She responded eagerly, shivering in his arms as her body tried to accommodate the surfeit of pleasure, too much, too fast.

Rafe dragged his parted lips slowly down her throat, exciting nerve endings, leaving a trail of fire in his wake. His mouth went down to her chest, and within the confinement of her bodice, she felt the tips of her breasts turn hard and sensitive. "Hannah," he whispered, spreading feverish kisses across her skin, "I've never wanted anyone this much before. You're so beautiful in every way . . . and everything I find out about you makes me love you more . . ." He lifted his head and gave it a rough shake as if to recall himself to where he was. A self-mocking grin came to his lips. "My God. We'd better make this a short betrothal. Here, give me your hand—no, the other." He searched one of the coat pockets and unearthed a shining circlet. It was a garnet set in silver. "This is why I went to the village today," he said, slipping the ring onto her fourth finger. "I'll buy you a diamond in London, but we had to start out with something."

"It's perfect," Hannah said, looking down at it with shining eyes. "A garnet means enduring love. Did you know that?"

He shook his head, staring at her as if she were a miracle.

Wrapping her arms around his neck, Hannah impulsively kissed him. Rafe angled his head over hers, possessing her lips with soft erotic demand. She ran her hands over the powerful lines of his body in a timid but ardent exploration, until she felt him shiver.

Gasping, he held her back from him. "Hannah . . . sweetheart, I'm . . . I've reached my limits. We have to stop."

"I don't want to stop."

"I know, love. But I have to escort you back inside before everyone notices that we're missing."

Everything in her rebelled at the thought of returning to the large, crowded ballroom. The talking, dancing, the long formal supper . . . it would be torture, when all she wanted was to be with him. Daringly, Hannah reached out to toy with the buttons of his waistcoat. "Take me to the bachelor's house. I'm sure it's empty. Everyone is at the manor."

He gave her a sardonic glance. "If I did that, sweetheart, there is no way you would get out of there with your innocence intact."

"I want you to compromise me," she told him.

"You do? Why, love?"

"Because I want to be yours in every way."

"You already are," he murmured.

"Not that way. Not yet. And even if you don't compromise me, I'm going to tell everyone that you did. So you may as well do it in actuality."

Rafe laughed at her threat. "In America," he told her, "we would say you're trying to seal the deal." Gently he framed her face in his hands, and stroked her cheeks with his thumbs. "But you don't have to, sweetheart.

There's nothing on earth that will keep me from marrying you. You can trust me."

"I do trust you. But . . ."

His brows lifted. "But?"

The skin beneath his fingers warmed a few degrees. "I want you. I want to be close to you. As . . . as you wrote in the letter."

He gave her one of those slow smiles that sent hot and cold chills down her spine. "In that case . . . maybe I'll compromise you just a little."

Pulling Hannah up from the bench, Rafe took her with him to the bachelor's house. He argued with himself every step of the way, knowing the right thing to do was to take her back to the manor without delay. And yet the desire to be alone with her, to hold her in privacy, was simply too powerful and all-encompassing to resist.

They went inside the bachelor's house, with its dark, stately furniture and paneled walls and luxurious rugs. Coals glowed in the bedroom hearth, spreading a pool of yellow and orange across the floor.

Rafe lit a bedside lamp and turned it low, and turned to look at Hannah. She had shed his coat and was reaching back to unfasten her ballgown. He saw her expression, how she was trying to appear nonchalant as if going to bed with a man were a normal occurrence for her. And he was filled with amusement and tenderness, and the most unholy ache of lust he'd ever experienced.

He went to her and reached around her, closing his hands over hers. "You don't have to do this," he said. "I'll wait for you. I'll wait as long as I have to."

Hannah tugged her hands free and slipped them behind his neck. "I can't think of a thing I'd rather be doing," she told him.

He bent to kiss her compulsively, pausing only to murmur, "Oh, love, neither can I."

Slowly he removed layers of silk and linen, and unhooked her corset, and rolled the stockings from her legs. When every last garment was gone, and she was stretched blushing on the bed before him, he let his gaze wander along her slender body, and he let out a shaking sigh. She was so beautiful, so innocent and trusting. He touched her breast, molding the softness with fingers that held a slight tremor.

Her gaze lifted to his face. "Are you nervous?" she asked with a touch of surprise.

Rafe nodded, brushing the pad of his thumb over a pink nipple and watching it tighten. "It's never been an act of love for me before."

"Does that make it different?"

A wry smile curved his lips as he considered that. "I'm not certain. But there's one way to find out."

He undressed himself and lay beside her, gathering her carefully in his arms. Despite the desire raging through his body, he pressed her against him with controlled gentleness, letting her feel him. He slid one hand over her bottom, rubbing in a warm circle.

Her breath caught as she felt the length of him against her. A small hand came to the surface of his chest and explored delicately. "Rafe . . . how should I touch you?"

He smiled and kissed her throat, savoring the softness and female fragrance of her. "Anywhere, love.

Any way you like." He held still as she played with the light pelt of hair on his chest.

Staring into his eyes, she let her palm drift to the muscles of his abdomen, stroking until they tightened reflexively. She fumbled a little as she grasped his aroused flesh, the hard satiny length alive and pulsing with masculine need. She gave him a few hesitant caresses. His response was so acute that he gasped at the sharply climbing sensation. "Hannah," he managed to say, reaching down to pull her hand away. "Change of plan. Next time"—he paused, struggling for self-control—"you can explore to your heart's content, but for now, let me make love to you."

"Did I do something wrong? Did you not like the way I—"

"I liked it too much. If I liked it any more, this would all be over in less than a minute." He rose above her and pressed kisses over her body, lingering at her breasts to tug and tease and softly bite. He delighted in the shocks of response he felt in her, the deepening color of arousal, the instinctive way she moved toward him to follow the source of pleasure.

Nudging her thighs open, he rested his hand between them, fitting his palm over the fleecy triangle. And he held her gently until she writhed and moaned, needing more. Sliding downward, Rafe kissed her stomach, letting his tongue trace delicate circles around her navel. He had never been so aroused, so completely absorbed in someone else's pleasure. The intimacy was nearly unbearable. His breathing was quick and frayed as he found the entrance of her body and teased around it with his fingertip.

"Hannah, darling," he whispered, "relax for me." He eased his finger inside the lush, clinging heat. The feel of her was so exquisite, he let out a groan. "I have to kiss you here. I have to taste you. No, don't be afraid . . . just let me . . . oh, Hannah, sweet love . . ." He dragged his mouth straight through the curls, and searched hungrily until he found the blunt silken peak. His senses were engulfed in radiant pleasure, all his muscles taut with lust. The taste of her, salt and female, was insanely arousing. He drew his tongue over her, flicked and circled, glorying in her helpless cries. He slid his finger deeper, and again, teaching her the rhythm.

She reached down with a low cry, her hands gripping his head. With tender skill he urged her into climax, luxuriating in the soft, pulsing warmth of her body. Long after her release had faded, he stayed with her, drawing his tongue through the rosy heat, easing her into a dreamy afterglow.

"Rafe," she said thickly, pulling him upward.

Smiling, he levered his body over hers, staring down into her dazed green eyes.

"More," she whispered, and wrapped her arms around his back, holding him to her. "I want more of you."

Murmuring her name, Rafe lowered his body into the cradle of her thighs. A rush of primitive satisfaction went through him as he felt the enticing softness parting for him. He pushed into the resisting flesh, so hot, so wet, and the deeper he went, the more tightly she closed around him. He thrust deep and held, trying not to hurt her. It was like nothing he had ever felt before, a pleasure beyond imagining. He took her head in his hands and kissed her mouth, while his senses swam in rapture. "I'm sorry, love," he said in a guttural voice. "So sorry to hurt you."

Hannah smiled and drew him down to her. "As a foreigner goes to a new country . . ." she whispered against his ear.

He let out a shaken laugh. "God. You'll never let me forget that letter, will you?"

"I never even read the whole thing," she said. "Parts of it were burned. And now I'll never know everything you said."

"The passages you missed were probably about this," he murmured, pushing gently inside her. They both caught their breath and held still, absorbing the feel of it. Rafe pressed a smile against her cheek. "I wrote quite a lot about this."

"Tell me what you wrote."

He whispered into her ear, love words and intimate praise, and all the longing he'd felt. And with each word he felt something opening inside him, a sense of freedom and power and perishing tenderness. She moved with him, welcoming him deeper, and the ecstasy of being joined with her roared through him, driving him to a piercing, brilliantly transcending release.

Indeed . . . love made it different.

Rafe held her for a long time afterward, his hand stroking gently over her back and hip. He couldn't seem to stop touching her. Hannah snuggled in the crook of his arm, her body feeling heavy and sated. "Is this real?" she whispered. "It feels like a dream."

Amusement rumbled in his chest. "It will seem real enough tomorrow morning when I take you back to the manor a fallen woman. If I hadn't already told Westcliff of my intentions to marry you, I daresay he'd greet me with a horsewhip."

"You aren't taking me back tonight?" she asked in pleased surprise.

"No. For one thing, I've ruined your coiffure. Second, I don't have the energy to leave this bed. Third . . . there's a distinct possibility that I'm not finished with you yet."

"Those are all very good reasons." She sat up and pulled the remaining pearl pins from her hair, and leaned over Rafe to deposit them on the bedside table. Catching her ribs in his hands, he held her over him and kissed her breasts as they were displayed before him. "Rafe," she protested.

Pausing, he looked up into her blushing face, and he grinned. "Modest?" he asked softly, and tucked her into the crook of his arm again. His lips pressed against her forehead. "Well. Being married to me will cure you of that soon enough."

Hannah leaned her face against his chest, and he felt the curve of her smile.

"What is it?" he asked.

"Our first night together. And our first morning will be Christmas."

Rafe patted her naked hip. "And I've already unwrapped my present."

"You're rather easy to shop for," she said, making him laugh.

"Always. Because Hannah, my love, the only gift I'll ever want"—he paused to kiss her smiling lips—"is you."

EPILOGUE

On Christmas morning Matthew Swift walked over to the bachelor's house, his shoes and the hem of his coat dusted with new snow. He knocked at the door and waited patiently until Rafe came to answer it. And with a wry smile, Swift told his brother-in-law, "All I can say is, everyone's talking. So you'd better marry her quickly."

There was, of course, no argument on Rafe's part.

Swift also told him that having been moved by the spirit of the holiday (and the combined pressuring of the entire family), Thomas Bowman had reconsidered his decision to disinherit Rafe, and wished to make peace. Later, over mugs of smoking bishop, a hot drink made with fruit, red wine, and port, the men came to an accord of sorts.

But Rafe did not consent to enter into the joint proprietorship with his father, realizing that the arrangement would undoubtedly be a source of future conflict between them. Instead, he entered into a highly lucrative partnership with Simon Hunt and Westcliff, and turned his abilities to the manufacturing of locomotive engines. This removed much of the burden from Hunt's shoulders, which made Annabelle happy, and allowed Rafe and Hannah to stay in England, to the pleasure of all.

In future years, Thomas Bowman would forget that Hannah was not the daughter-in-law he had originally wanted for Rafe, and a solid affection developed between them.

Natalie married Lord Travers and they were very happy together. She confided to Hannah that when she had gone to Travers for consolation that Christmas Eve, he had finally kissed her, and it had been a kiss worth waiting for.

Daisy eventually finished her novel, which was published with great popular success, if not critical acclaim.

Evie gave birth later that year to a high-spirited girl with flame-colored curls, leading St. Vincent to the conclusion that it was his destiny to be loved by many red-haired women. He was very pleased.

Hannah and Rafe were married by the end of January, but they always considered their true anniversary to be Christmas, and celebrated accordingly. And every Christmas Eve, Rafe wrote a love letter and left it on her pillow.

Samuel Clark hired a new secretarial assistant, a competent and pleasant young woman. Upon discovering her auspiciously shaped cranium, he married her without delay.

In 1848, a woodcut of the Queen and Prince Albert standing beside their Christmas tree was published in *The Illustrated London News,* popularizing the custom until soon every parlor was graced with a decorated tree. After viewing the illustration, Lillian rather smugly observed that her tree was much taller.

Thomas Bowman's toupee, alas, was never found. He was somewhat mollified by the gift of a very fine hat from Westcliff on Christmas Day.

AUTHOR'S NOTE

Dear Friends,

I hope you've enjoyed visiting the fictional world of the Wallflowers! Writing this story was a delightful experience for many reasons. I loved being able to include research about Victorian Christmas facts and traditions, and most of all, I had fun spending time with characters I had "lived with" for a number of years. When I create characters, I spend a lot of time developing their backgrounds, and pondering how their experiences form their hopes, dreams, and perceptions about the world. But I truly start learning about a character when I put him into situations with other people. I've come to realize that in fiction and in real life, every encounter we have with another person, no matter how fleeting, has the potential to change us . . . the way we think, the decisions we'll make in the future.

What I love most about writing a series is seeing the progression of characters from book to book, and as I revisit them, I have the feeling of spending time with old friends. The Wallflower series, the Hathaways, and the Travises have all been rewarding and fulfilling experiences for me as an author. It is my earnest hope that my readers have found similar enjoyment in visiting these fictional worlds with me.

Now I've started working on a new series, with a set of characters I'm still becoming acquainted with. The Friday Harbor series takes place in the San Juan Islands, which are part of Washington State—I can't imagine a more beautiful or vibrant setting for a novel. The series centers on the Nolan brothers, who have to learn that there is more to being a family than mere blood ties. As I follow them through these upcoming novels, exploring themes of love, family, loyalty, and commitment, I hope you'll come along for the ride.

We'll meet some of these new characters in the soon-to-be-released *Christmas Eve at Friday Harbor*, when the oldest Nolan brother, Mark, becomes the guardian of his orphaned niece Holly. In her letter to Santa, Holly asks for just one thing . . . a new mom for Christmas. As Mark struggles to create a family for Holly, his life goes in directions he never anticipated, and he discovers that sometimes the heart has a will of its own . . .

Thank you as always for your kindness and encouragement—my readers always inspire me to search my heart and try to do my very best!

Wishing you happiness always,

Lisa

Take a sneak peek at Lisa Kleypas's latest novel

CHRISTMAS EVE
AT FRIDAY HARBOR

Coming in hardcover in October 2010
from St. Martin's Press

CHAPTER ONE

Three weeks before Christmas, Mark found the letter.

It had been left in a pile on the table in Halle's play-room, tucked into an envelope made with Scotch tape, construction paper, and glittery star stickers.

Dear Santa,
I think I am on the nice list. I don't want any presents this year except for one thing. I need a new mom. I may not get one because I heard nowadays its hard to find a good woman. But if you know one, please drop her off at Friday Harbor.

Love,
Halle
P.S. I was going to talk to you when you were here last week but my uncle Mark said the line was too long.

"Damn it," Mark whispered. He read the letter again, an eight-year-old girl's Christmas wish for something that every child deserved. A mother.

He wasn't ready for the bolt of pain that shot through his chest. That was the strange thing about grieving—even when you thought you'd gotten over the worst of it, it could still hit you just as hard as it did the first moment you heard the words *she's gone*.

He'd gotten that call six months ago.

"I'm so sorry . . . I'm a friend of Virginia and Phil's, I'm watching over Halle and the police just called and . . ." The babysitter had started crying, forcing out words between sobs, and it took a minute or two for Mark to understand that his sister and her husband had been in a car wreck in Seattle. Their sedan had hydroplaned and crossed into oncoming traffic, where they'd been broadsided. They had both died instantly.

There had been a feeling of unreality about the situation, a layer of numbness covering a reservoir of pain that Mark had no idea how to deal with. Nolans didn't do well with loss, any more than they knew what to do with happiness. In a family that had not exactly been equipped for emotional closeness, Virginia had been the only one who had managed to draw them all together on occasion. Mark had been fine with seeing Virginia and his younger brother Sam during the obligatory once-a-year get-together at Christmas. Other than that, he sent e-mails or texted once in a blue moon. He had seen no point in sharing their lives with each other.

Virginia's death had changed everything.

His sister had neglected to mention to Mark that she and Phil had named him as Halle's guardian if anything ever happened to them. As a man who hated to be tied down, who enjoyed his fast-paced and disposable lifestyle, Mark was the last man on the planet who should have been named as anyone's guardian. It was Halle's rotten luck, however, that he was her best option, the other potential guardian being Sam.

"You're not actually going to keep her, are you?" Sam had asked at the reception after the funeral.

Mark had scowled at him. "Of course I'm going to keep her. What the hell else am I supposed to do?"

"Give her to someone else."

"Like who? Phil's parents are too old to look after a kid."

"Maybe one of the cousins could take her. There's Carla and her husband . . . what's his name . . ."

"Divorced."

"Damn." Sam's mouth was grim. "No offense, bro, but you're not exactly the dad type. You could screw up what's left of her childhood."

"Since both her parents are dead, I'd say her chances of having a great childhood are pretty well screwed by now."

They talked in undertones that cut beneath the subdued conversation of the mourners. Guests filled their plates at the buffet table, serving spoons clinking against chafing dishes, drinks being poured. From time to time someone laughed quietly at some shared memory. Tissues were pressed gently against eyes and noses. The rituals of mourning were being observed, and while it seemed to bring comfort to the people around him, it did nothing for Mark.

He had slid covert glances at Halle, who was sitting

at a table on the other side of the room with a book. Her soft brown hair, usually neatly braided, was drawn back in an off-center ponytail. Already the loss of a mother was showing. Mark had gone through her closet that morning and had found nothing that looked appropriate for a funeral. Half her wardrobe consisted of sparkly ballgowns, and the other half was bright T-shirts and embroidered jeans.

Halle had been surrounded by women who fussed over her and brought her little plates of food as she sat at a table with a book. Countless slips of paper with phone numbers had been pressed into Mark's hand, with offers of "help with Halle." One had insisted on entering her number into his iPhone. "You're not alone, Mark," she had told him meaningfully.

More than a few female gazes were drawn to the pair of Nolan brothers standing in the corner. Neither of the brothers was precisely handsome, but both had looks that carried. They were big-framed and dark-haired, rough-natured but soft-spoken in the way of native-born islanders. Mark was the only one who'd ever moved away from San Juan Island, staying in Seattle after he'd graduated from U-Dub.

The city was only a ferry ride or a half-hour flight from Friday Harbor, but it was a world away. Mark loved Seattle, the gray winter downpours and lemon-colored summers, the culture of books and coffee, the restaurants that always told you where and when the fish was caught. And he loved the spectacular variety of women, stylish, smart, sexy, funny. He had no desire to commit to any particular woman. He wasn't just afraid of commitment, he was allergic to it.

Now, apparently, he was settling down with some-one whether he was ready or not.

And she was five.

It had been enough to make Mark panic. Except that when he looked across the room at his niece, the enor-mity of her loss, her aloneness, had hit him like a ton of bricks. Halle had no choice about what was happening to her. But Mark did have a choice, and for once in his life, he was going to try to do the right thing. It was ob-vious that he was going to be a rotten parent, but maybe that was still better for Halle than being shoved off on strangers.

And then Mark had looked at Sam, and it had oc-curred to him that Sam owed her just as much as he did. "We're a family," he had heard himself saying.

Sam had looked at him blankly.

"You, me, and Halle," Mark had said. "There's only the three of us. We should do this together."

"Do what together? You mean . . . you want me to help you raise Halle? Jesus, Mark. *No*. Not happening."

"Why not?"

"I don't know anything about kids."

"Neither do I."

"We're not really a family," Sam had said. "I'm pretty sure I don't even like you."

"Tough luck," Mark said, gaining confidence in the idea. "If I'm doing this, you're helping me. Halle and I are moving in with you at Rainshadow. There's plenty of room."

Sam lived on San Juan Island in a big Victorian coun-try house, running the vineyard and winery their father had started more than thirty years earlier. The place was named after the rainshadow cast by the Olympic Mountains, which spared the island much of the drizzle and grayness that surged over the rest of the Pacific Northwest.

Of the group of islands that formed an archipelago belonging to Washington State, San Juan was the farthest from the mainland. The air was dry and weighted with ocean salt, sweetened by the lavender harvests in summer. It was an easygoing, bare-limbed, full-flowered island, a place where bald eagles looped from tree to tree, and resident pods of orcas swam and fed and sometimes drifted lazily with the tide.

"There may be room in the house," Sam had said, "but not in my life. You're not bringing her there, Mark." Seeing the intractable look on his brother's face, he had cursed softly and said, "You're going to do it anyway, aren't you?"

"Yeah, I'm going to do it. Just for a while." He had sighed shortly at Sam's expression. "Damn it, Sam, help me get through this beginning part. Halle and I don't even know each other."

"And you think Friday Harbor's a better place to raise her than Seattle?" Sam had asked skeptically.

"Yes," Mark had replied without hesitation. "I've got to slow things down. Living on island time is better for both of us."

"What about your business?"

"Seattle's only a half-hour flight from Friday Harbor. I can go back and forth."

They were both quiet for a minute. Sam looked around Mark at Halle's downbent head. She was methodically picking raisins out of cookies and making a little pile on her plate. "Poor kid," Sam whispered. "How do you think we're going to pull this off, Mark?"

"Like the saying goes . . . fake it so real you're beyond fake."

Usually when your life went in a new direction, you had some kind of warning. You got to think it over, try it on for size, back out if it wasn't working. With a child . . . with Halle . . . there was no backing out. Which meant the only thing left to do was give it their best shot. They had made it through six months of painful holidays . . . Halle's first birthday without parents, the first Halloween, the first Thanksgiving without every place at the family table filled. Mark thought they were doing okay.

Until the letter.

. . . I don't want any presents this year except for one thing. I need a new mom.

"You realize what this means," Mark told Sam after Halle had gone to bed that night.

"That we stink as parents," Sam said, staring morosely at the glittering envelope in his hand. "She needs a woman in her life. Maybe we should find her a nanny."

"It means," Mark said quietly, "one of us needs to get married."